the realm of possibility

the
realm
of
possibility

david levithan

Alfred A. Knopf New York

Special thanks to Susan Fromm for her claddagh ring

THIS IS A BORZOI BOOK PUBLISHED BY ALFRED A. KNOPF

Text copyright © 2004 by David Levithan

www.randomhouse.com/teens

Library of Congress Cataloging-in-Publication Data
Levithan, David.
The realm of possibility / David Levithan.
p. cm.
SUMMARY: A variety of students at the same high school describe
their ideas, experiences, and relationships in a series of interconnected
free-verse stories.
ISBN 0-375-82845-1 (trade) — ISBN 0-375-92845-6 (lib. bdg.)
[1. Interpersonal relations—Fiction. 2. Conduct of life—Fiction. 3. High
schools—Fiction. 4. Schools—Fiction.] I. Title.
PZ7.L5798Re2004
[Fic]—dc22
2003061917

Printed in the United States of America
August 2004
10 9 8 7 6 5 4 3 2 1

For Billy
(for the poetry of his friendship)

Acknowledgments

I have been graced with so many possibilities, it is impossible for me to thank everyone who's helped shine the way to this book. Once again, it started as a valentine to my friends. And once again, it belongs to them and my wonderful family, particularly my amazing parents.

Many people helped me as I made my way through these pages. Billy Merrell, Eireann Corrigan, Jinny Wolff, and Dar Williams continue to inspire me with their words and music. Dan Poblocki, Ed Spade, Laura Heston, Michael Renehan, Nico Medina, Brian Selznick, David Serlin, Joe Monti, Cary Retlin, Jennifer Bodner, David Leventhal, Mike Rothman, and Patrick Flanery were all instrumental during the drafting of these lines. Everyone at Knopf has been a dream to work with, especially Amy Ehrenreich, Melody Meyer, and Melissa Nelson. And my colleagues and writers at Scholastic still teach me how to do it, every day.

Without Nancy Mercado, this book would have never begun. Thank you for lighting the first match.

Nancy Hinkel makes me the luckiest guy on the Lower East Side. Or anywhere else, for that matter.

The word "unlonely" comes to me from Eddie de Oliveira's fantastic novel *Lucky*. "Possibility" was finished just hours after the commitment ceremony of my friends Jen Corn and Roo Cline. I hope it contains at least some of the glory of that day.

the realm of possibility

one

Daniel

Mary

Diana

Megan

smoking

i've never smoked a cigarette
with anyone but jed.
senior year, driver's licenses,
our town is so many miles
with nowhere to go.
nowhere but the woods,
where leaves block out the haze of the city
blocking out the stars.
we pass the cigarette hand to hand, and
somehow i can see the trail of smoke in the
darkness. the way i can see jed's eyes
even when there isn't any light.

it would never have occurred to me to smoke.
but one day we're at the 7-11 and jed says *buy a pack*.
we have been in the 7-11 for twenty minutes
reading newsprint about bat boy and the
shocking! gay! love! affair! of someone
in hollywood, and jed jokes that if our local
paper was like that, we'd certainly be
headline news.

i have never wanted to be a cowboy
but i ask for marlboros anyway.
i have to prove myself

2

with the photo that doesn't really look like me,
only a department of motor vehicles version.
i don't know whether to smile
and it shows. i thank the shopguy like
he's delivered the cigarettes to my door.
it's only when we're back in the car that
jed asks me if i got matches.
I am so new at this.

jed is not a smoker
but he's smoked.
i am not a smoker
and i have never smoked.
i light matches for candles
for sitting in my room and wanting
a flicker of life, a flicker of mood.
the smoke i've known is
vanilla scented.

i think he will laugh but instead
he tells me he loves the way i am.
hearing those words is like
being handed flowers. we walk
to the woods and find the one bench,
our hidden observation post.
as we sit on the carved names of other discoverers
he takes the cellophane from the pack,
smoothes it between his fingers,
and folds it into a ring.

i open the cardboard,
pull out a cigarette, slightly amazed
at how light it is. like a piece of chalk
made of paper.

jed and i don't have much in common.
he is much stronger than i think i am. he is
mischievous, outgoing, ready to soar
through clouds while i often feel
like the cloud itself. we are a strange pair
and we love that. we've been going
to school together since sixth grade
but we didn't really meet until last year's art class.
we had both drawn escher patterns on our jeans.
do you like magritte? he asked
and at first i didn't really know jed was
although i was sure he knew that i was
but gradually we both knew
and we knew.

i hold the cigarette like i'm in a black-and-white movie.
but when jed lights the match, it spreads to color,
his skin in the campfire light, the spark of his eyes
as he leans in to me. *when the match touches,*
he says, *breathe it in.* i wait for the glow,
the yellow smoldering to orange. i wait
and then i inhale. one long drag as jed shakes off
the match. i can taste the dark spice of the smoke.
i take it in too long, too fast. my body says *not yet*

and pushes the smoke back out in a cough. i feel
foolish, but jed smiles and says i'm doing fine,
better than he did. he takes the cigarette
from my hand, brings the orange deeper, then
hands it back to me and says *try again.*

my parents are okay with me being gay
but they would kill me if they saw me with
a cigarette. which makes sense, in a way.
my friend pete would also have something
to say. he says his body is a temple, and i think
that's the problem with the two of us lately. i don't want
my body to be a temple. i don't want it to be
worshiped or congregated. pete is an athlete
and my next door neighbor and we've known
each other so long that we can talk about anything
except jed. or what pete calls
that whole thing.

the second breath works. the smoke
fills my air. it doesn't feel good or bad
just a buzz of different. we sit down and pass it
back and forth. it is hard for us to be alone
between school and our friends and our families
and his track practice and my literary magazine.
so this pause is heaven, feeling entirely
open. we talk and sit close and the only
time that passes is the ash that falls.
i have never had anybody talk to me like this.

this is not a flirty sixth-grade phone call or
bantering with friends or words passed in a note.
i feel that if my soul could talk it would
talk like this.

i am willing to smoke the cigarette until
it disappears. jed tells me when it's time to stop.
i reach into the pack for another but jed
says one is enough. anyone can do more,
but it will be our thing to do just one.
we talk until our voices are tired
and then we talk about what we're doing
tomorrow. when i get home, the pack safely hidden
in the trunk of my car, i am surprised
to find that my hand still smells like smoke.
i know i should wash it, hide it too, but
the scent makes me think of him.
so i let it linger.

it becomes one of our rituals. like
skipping sixth period study hall together
like signing our notes with *truth beauty freedom love.*
these things let us know how we fit
with each other, even if we aren't sure
how we fit with everybody else.
i look at guys like pete and sometimes feel
lost. he works out for two and a half hours a day.
he has this perfection he wants to be.
he travels in groups and looks so at ease.

even though i know him well enough
to know he gets nervous and tries
too hard, i still look at him sometimes and
think that's the way jed and i should be.

when i am with jed, though, i don't
care. we head to the soccer field for
our second cigarette. beyond the goals,
far from the school. we don't hold hands
until we're out of view, but that gives it
more of a charge. we can still hear people's
voices, but they can't hear ours. we talk
about growing up, about college. jed
talks about *the foreseeable future* and
how little there is that we can foresee.
which gives the present more of a charge.
inhaling deeply, i am aware that something
touching my lips has just touched
his. so uncomplicated.

i can't pretend to know
how to smoke. i just do it.
i can't pretend to know
what love is. it just is.

because it is senior year i have begun to see things
as potential absences. the things i love will become
the things i'll miss. i don't know how to use this
negative sight. when jed and i are playful i feel very

young. when jed and i are serious i feel
older, like how I feel when I'm wearing a suit.
when i was twelve, smoking a cigarette would have
made me feel old. when i am forty, maybe smoking
will make me feel young. but right now all it makes me
feel is that i am with jed and we are in the same place
and time. when we kiss
we taste the same.

pete comes over to do homework later that night
and he tells me my shirt smells like a concert and asks me
if i went to see a band without him. i tell him
i barely recognize his body from all the working out and he takes it
as a compliment. tells me how much he's lifting and how much more
he'd like it to be. i have known him since we were small enough
to fit in a kiddie pool. i have heard about the girls
he's made out with and he's heard about all the girls
i didn't quite. back before i thought of friendship in terms of love,
i would've never said we loved each other. and now
that i think of friendship in terms of love,
i'm still not sure.

the first time jed asked me on a date i almost
cried. this was in the middle of junior year. having
someone think of me that way was like discovering
a new window in the room i'd lived in all my life.
in my english notebook, i had cataloged his graces
while in his mind he had detailed my kindnesses,
dreamed about saying things i dreamed of hearing.

he had been seeing someone and i had seen a lot of people
from afar. we realized the only thing separating us
was air. we walked through it with simple words.
we knew that all we had to do was tell two people
for the whole school to know. so we told two people
and were a little surprised when nothing happened
except our surprise. we were okay, i think, because
we kept to ourselves. which was exactly where
we wanted to be.

i drive around and smile when i think of the cigarettes
in the trunk. one time my mother needs to borrow the car
and i spend the whole day nervous that she'll crush them
with her groceries, discover them and turn on me
with questions. jed teases me all day and then
when we get the car back he insists there's a cigarette
missing, that my mother has stolen one from us on the sly.
i've lost count—are we on seven or eight?—it
no longer matters. we sit on our bench and listen for owls
and i feel like i am at home in the world.

we make it to the last cigarette, proud
of ourselves for sticking to our plan. it is a sunday night,
television hour, and we are fugitives
in the park after sundown. i light the match this time
as jed inhales. and i, who have never thought
in terms of a life, think to myself that
i could make a life out of this.
not the smoking, but the aura of smoking,

the togetherness and the nightfall and the words
that we share. *i could make a life out of this.*
i, who have never been prepared.

we are quiet tonight, but in the same
silence. we hear the footsteps together,
too many of them, and loud. i can tell from the way they walk,
the way that jed and i don't really walk,
that they're guys from our school. and i am
scared. in a way that jed is not scared.
it's not until they're closer, until they're seeing us,
that i realize one of them is pete.
one of the guys says, *what's this?* and pete
just looks at me. i say hello, ask him
what's up. and all he can say back to me is
you're smoking?

he says this seriously and i
laugh. he doesn't join me and i feel us
becoming untied. the guys move on, one or two of them
making jokes about me and jed, about *interrupting.*
pete does not look back. he's walking away and at the same time
i feel like i'm the one leaving him behind. i realize
i have already made a life out of this. i am capable
of making a life. i pass the cigarette to jed after taking
one last drag. he asks me if i'm okay and i say i'm
more than that. he agrees, and wipes some ash from my shirt.
the night continues, and we continue. i fold
the empty pack of cigarettes in my pocket, to keep.

once time is lit, it will burn
whether or not you're breathing it in.
even after smoke becomes air
there is the memory of smoke.

i am seeing, as if by the light of a match,
a glimpse of my life
and having it feel right.

this will linger.

tinder heart

i.

don't touch me
i said
because i can't
handle
someone being
good to me.

he heard me
and he listened
and i thought
my body would cry
from all it felt
and all it couldn't.

he leaned
on the pillow
and i missed him
so i curled into
his side and stroked
his arm. i didn't
mind touching him.
he was solid.
he was there

as i dissolved.
why do you
do this?
he asked.
even though
i wasn't sure
what he meant
i said
i don't know
because that
had become
my answer
to everything.

ii.

there is
negative noticing
and there is
positive noticing.
i walk the hallway with
my friend elizabeth
and i can't help
but hate her
because she doesn't care
if they notice
(negatively)

or if they notice
(positively)
and i hate myself
because i can't help
caring, looking to see
if they notice
and what they think.

you can see
her bra strap
it's practically
at her neck
and because of this
i'm not listening
as she asks me
about last night
about pete
and what he means
to me. she doesn't like
how big he is or
how little i am
even though
she doesn't care
what shape she's in
or whether her
bra strap is showing
for all the world to
ignore.
three boys pass

without seeing me.
i should be glad
but instead
i'm the opposite.
the negative.

iii.

he intercepts me
outside the cafeteria.
we'd been at his house
which meant i was
the one to leave.
and as i walked home
i imagined him
on the couch
still reaching for me
still touching air.

how are you?
he asks.
no *hello*
no greeting kiss
for me to avoid.
no, he wants to
know how i am
and i can't stop

thinking
you care
too much—
don't you know
i'm bound
to leave
you?

he reaches into
his bag. he rustles
and digs and
rummages until
finally
he takes out
all his books
to find me
a crushed
paper crane
that his sister
has made.
a thousand
for peace
and one
for me.

look at it
fly, he says,
but before
he can send it

through the halls,
i touch
his arm and
he puts it
in my hands
and puts his
fingers under mine,
cupping the crane
as he says it
again,
look at it
fly.

iv.

who was it
who invented
size zero?

who was it
who promised
that if you got
to a certain point
you would no
longer
be?

v.

his body is
unbelievable.
then i am
touching it
and i believe.

he used to
believe too
but i think
being with me
has made him
lose some of
his faith. we
are lying there
and he says
out of the blue
*i miss being
ticklish.
i would laugh
at anything.*
he moves to
tickle me.
i know he's
being playful,
but i knock
his hand away.
i tell him to

stop it.
he says
it used to
be fun. then
he says
i worry
about you
and i tell him
don't
and he says
that's exactly
why.

vi.

at the mall
elizabeth says
is that all
you're eating?
and i tell her
i'm having dinner
later and she says,
mary, it's nine.
and i tell her
i'm okay and
she says *that*
wasn't my

question and
i say *you know*
it was and she
says *that's true.*
i just wanted
to see if you
knew it,
too.

vii.

why won't they
leave me
alone?
don't they
realize i
have a
tinder heart
and a
paper body
and that
any spark
will turn me
straight to
ash?

viii.

he takes me
driving.
he looks
nervous
and i wonder
if he's taking
me out to the
woods to
dump me.

they might
never find
the body,
i joke. he laughs
but it's a laugh
he has to
think about
first.

we have a
spot at an
overlook.
we always
stop there
to take in
the hilly view.
sometimes

the picnic bench
has families,
other times
drunks or bikers,
but this time
it's waiting
just for us.

pete takes out
a basket of
food and
two beers.
I nibble at
the crackers
and try not to
think about them.
we are a nice
couple on a nice
date.

we talk about
gossip and
parents and
exams and
then he says
he has something
to tell me, and what
he has to tell me
is that i am

not happy, not
healthy, that i
need help.

it is not him
talking. these
are not the kind
of words he
uses. *who put
you up to this?*
i yell. *who are you
doing this for?*
and he says
*i'm doing it
for you.*

i get mad. i
am screaming
at him that he's
no better, that
he's as trapped
in his body
as i am and that
if he thinks
all of his working
out and obsession
about his body
is any different
than what i worry

about then he's
stupid and deluded.

and he says
you're right,
and he says
i made him
realize this
before i even
said a word.
and he says
he doesn't
know what
to do and i
suggest he just
give up on me
and he says
that's not
an option.

i tell him
i want to go
home. he stares
for a second,
takes me in,
then says if
that's what i want,
we can. when we
get back i storm

out of the car
and slam the door
and when my mom
asks me what's wrong
i realize i can't tell
anybody about this
because i know
they'll all agree
with him.

ix.

i want
him to
give up.

no.

no, i
don't.

x.

he starts
working out

less, only
at practice,
only when
it's expected.
not for me,
but because
of me.
he says
it's a matter
of priorities
he'd gotten
wrong.

it's not his body
that changes
right away.
it's something
inside. he says
he wants to
be a little
weaker. i don't
understand.
i say *thinner?*
and he says
no, i want
to be stronger
in a different
way. not
because of me,
but for me.

xi.

elizabeth tells me
it's all my
decision.
then we
take out our
sketchbooks
and consider
a tulip
in her yard.

i can barely
lift
the pencil. i
feel that
weighed
down.

xii.

that night
i am
all alone
in the house.
my parents
have left me
for a movie.

pete is at
an away game.
elizabeth is
on a date.
so my whole
world is
this empty
house.

i could just
watch tv
write
some e-mail
but instead
i wander
the house
like a
ghost.

i run
my hands
over
the piano.
i score
the silence.
i tread
through air.
i feel
gone.

i feel
like the
shadow
behind the
shades.

from room
to room
my bare feet
on the
bare floor
my thoughts
are air
nowhere
nothing
is in me
with me
no moon
no night
i do not
turn on
the lights
everything
is where
i know it
to be
beyond
sight.

i end up
in the kitchen
i end up
in front of
the refrigerator
in front of
the door
i open
quietly
to be bathed
in the light
that would
startle
phantoms
the light
that makes me
glow
like a
midnight
visitation.

and i stand
there and i
wonder what
i am doing
i wonder
what
i
should

do
and i don't
know i
don't know
i don't know
what
to do
i don't
know whether
to take
to hold
to stay
to walk away
and i think
that is it—
that is
everything
and i sit
on the
kitchen tile
and i stare
into that
light with
all the plastic
colors behind it
all the
cold that
is not the
real air

all the feelings
are dead
inside me
and i
want them
to be
alive.

xiii.

at midnight
i am
at his
front door.
the question
he asks is
*why are you
so cold?*
and i say
*why are you
so warm?*
as he's
holding me
close
and he says
i just am
and still

i can't
say it.
i follow
him into
the den
quiet steps
so his parents
won't wake.
he holds
my hand
and when we
close the door
and lean into
the couch
all he wants
to do is
talk
but i put
my finger
to his lips
i tell him
to *shhhh*
i take off
his shirt
trace the
lines until
he pulls
me close
holds

me with
such caring
looks at me
with such
caring
such open
vulnerability
i know
he wants me
to be the one
who can break
him
but doesn't.

and when he
catches me
off guard
and says
i love you
i catch him
off guard
and say *i need your help.*

Love songs for Elizabeth

track one: something to you

there was a time before you
but I can't remember it now
a time before your beauty and I
were formally introduced
I'm sure I lived without you
but I don't remember how
can't imagine living without
these feelings you've produced

just one glance
and my life was redrawn
just one word
and my vocabulary changed
I asked the time
and you said *what's the hurry?*
you asked my name
and I almost forgot

I know
the odds are all against me
and I know
you might not feel this way too

but I know
I would rather die trying
to know
if I could mean something to you

seven wonders of the world
and I have to ask for an eighth
fill a bottle with some prayers
and spend them on hope
create an easy route
just so I can complicate
send my heart down that
slippery slope

we're on
our way to being friends
and I guess I'd
like to make a detour
you seem
to recognize me in the halls
you wave hello
and I lose all of my nerve

I know
the odds are all against me
and I know
you might not feel this way too
but I know
I would rather die trying

to know
if I could mean something to you

I want this world
small enough for the two of us
I want you to think of me
that way
I want this world
to crash us into marvelous
I want you to kiss me
and say:

I know
the odds are all against us
and I know
you feel this way too
so I know
I would rather die trying
to know
if I could mean something to you

[repeat last verse]

track two: you need a girl

Forget about the guys who never call.
Forget about the ones who set you up to see you fall.
Princes leave you at the ball.
Take a break from guys who never see—
Depressive jerks who want to say who you should be.
Find the one who'll set you free. . . .

You need a girl, need a girl, a girl who'll come through.
You need a girl, need a girl, a girl who needs you.

You've suffered through too many dates.
You've fended off the ones who only want to mate—
You're what they masturbate.
They'll never see you have a mind.
They'll always act like they're at least five years behind.
Never knowing to be kind.

You need a girl, need a girl, a girl who'll see you.
You need a girl, need a girl, a girl who needs you.

No more of the tired girl and boy.
All the methods that your parents will deploy
To keep you from your joy.
Find the one who clearly understands
That you don't have to land yourself a man.
Give your side a hand.

A girl, a girl, a girl

You'll be amazed at what you've found
With your spirits up and toilet seats placed face-down.
Embraces all around.
Sleep without that constant fear.
Silent struggles, being distant when you're near.
The answer is right here.

You need a girl, a girl, a girl who needs you.
You need a girl, a girl, a girl who loves you.
Right here . . .
Right here . . .

track three: my history

the first time I kissed someone
my heart raced for hours
I didn't know if I'd ever recover
if it was already too late.
I just lay in my room
and reveled in the newfound power
that a motion so small
could have the full force of fate.

it wasn't love that time
more like experimentation
I had to wait some time
for something more real.
some kisses I found
were pure lamentation
and other lips I touched
for something to feel.

you are not the first girl
that I have fallen for
and I know I'm not the first girl
that you'd ever choose.
you are not the first girl
to have led me to longing
but you could be the first girl
I don't manage to lose.

I'm not good at relationships
I always manage to find the flaws
sometimes in others
but mostly my own.
I foretell the ending
then go and create the cause
save myself
and end up alone.

the last time I kissed someone
my heart felt this loneliness
I didn't know if I'd ever recover
if it was already too late.
I just lay in my room
and wrestled with the emptiness
an emotion so big
it had the full force of fate.

you are not the first girl
that I have fallen for
and I know I'm not the first girl
that you'd ever choose.
you are not the first girl
to have led me to longing
but you could be the first girl
I don't manage to lose.

I'm telling you this
because you've made it different now.

I'm telling you this
because you caused something to live.
back came
the feelings I would not allow.
back came
my chances to give.

I'm not good at relationships
I always manage to find the flaws
sometimes in others
but mostly my own.
I foretell the ending
then go and create the cause
save myself
and end up alone.

you are not the first girl
that I have fallen for
and I know I'm not the first girl
that you'd ever choose.
you are not the first girl
to have led me to longing
but you could be the last girl
I don't manage to lose.

track four: open heart night

It's open heart night at the Claire d'Lune
and I'm hoping real bad just to see you soon
To see your face as you walk in the room
so I can wrestle you down with an open heart tune

If the spotlight's on me, will you look to the dark?
If I sing my arrow, will it hit its mark?

We all wait our turn to get up to the stage
Guitars at the ready for minimum wage
Just the chance to sing it like it never will be
Looking to unlock you with a major key

If I shout it, will you hear?
Can my chords bring you near?

Hear me, please hear me
Calling to you from open heart night
Come in, sit down
And be my audience tonight

I plug in my amp and scan the crowd
The din of the talking is growing so loud
Familiar faces are plain to see
But not the one that means it all to me

So is it that you've got other plans
Leaving me here with all the other also-rans?

It's open heart night at the Claire d'Lune
and I'm hoping real bad just to see you soon
You won't come when I call, but I'll call 'til you do
This open heart night won't ever be through
No, this open heart night won't ever be through

track five: the ride home

just when I think I'll never reach you
you see me and offer a ride
it's well past midnight, we're at the same party
I wasn't planning on leaving
but I do

as we're walking outside
I hear my friends fade behind me
megan saying *be careful*
alice saying *just go*
you unlock my door first
and ask how I'm doing
then say that you're sorry
you missed my show

the engine is revving
the headlights are beaming
and I find that I'm losing
my hold on the thread
that binds us together
that ties me so tightly
that keeps me attached to
the things left unsaid

we drive for miles
        and I get nowhere

we drive for miles
          in the dark
we drive for miles
          you're taking me home
we drive for miles
          in the dark

lit by the streetlamps
your face is a moonstone
the glow of the dashboard
seeps through my hand
you ask me some questions
and I give you some answers
but nothing that would make you
understand

the speedometer's counting
all of my chances
the radio is playing
songs I cannot sing
I am moving my hand
I'm crossing the distance
but leave it halfway
inexplicable thing

we drive for miles
          and I get nowhere
we drive for miles
          in the dark

we drive for miles
        you're taking me home
we drive for miles
        in the dark

your eyes on the road
you move your palm onto mine
you press down like salvation
then lighten your grip
a glimmer of smile
as we drive on together
I measure the moment
in the heartbeats I skip

it doesn't last long
the steering wheel turning
I see my house
as your hand retreats
you don't seem to realize
what it is that has happened
as you drop me off
on the side of the street

we drive for miles
        and I get lost
we drive for miles
        in the dark
we drive for miles
        you wish me a good night

we drive for miles
    in the dark

we drive for miles
    I follow your taillights
we drive for miles
    in the dark
we drive for miles
    and I'm left nowhere
we drive for miles
    in the dark

track six: thirty questions

what do I mean to you?
why are you mean to me?
is this a fantasy?
is anything real?
why can't I be with you?
what will you say to me?
why can't I walk away?
will you please stay?

why can't I fall for
someone who'll love me?
why isn't anything
I do good enough?
why does the sight of you
make me start trembling?
will you please be the one
to save me from you?

why did you hold my hand?
why won't I let you go?
who do you think you are,
to do this to me?
is it all over?
is it only beginning?
why do I miss you
when I see you each day?

how can I reach you
if you won't even notice?
how can you say that
he's even your type?
why do I long for you
when you are so wrong for me?
what is the purpose
of this kind of love?

does it ever get easier?
is there an end to these questions?
do you have any answers?
will you say them to me?
can you stop this unraveling?
will you bring me your closure?
or am I the only one
who sees anymore?
who sees . . .
who sees . . .
who sees?

track seven: it's all wrong

he brings you flowers on an orange tray
you pass him notes when he's not looking
he fills your bag with candy hearts
you feel him watching as you walk away

       it's all wrong
       I don't know how to hold it
       it's all wrong, today

you are asking me if I'm okay
then go on before I answer
you're telling me there will be someone
then tell me how he's brightened your day

            SEE THIS SCREAM—IT'S FOR YOU
            SEE THIS HURT—IT'S BY YOU
            SEE THIS MARK—IT'S FROM YOU
            but you don't see, no you don't see

       it's all wrong
       I don't know how to hold it in
       it's all wrong, today

I search out silent corners
stare at the blank pages
drink messages in bottles

make vows I always break
pretending to be happy
so hard it starts to hurt me
so loud no room is quiet
so silly because I know, of course I know

       it's all wrong
       there is no point in holding
       it's all wrong, today

I see the hurt
I see the mark
I see the signs
there's nothing I can do

       there is a time he'll say "I love you"
       there is a time you'll say "I love you" back

track eight: finale

All alone now.
Try to know how.
Reach for stars and touch the air.

I was made for this.
Nothing else but this.

Find the beauty.
Shirk the duty.
Trace the footsteps in the rain.

I have gone through this.
Nothing else but this.

Won't recover.
Lost a lover.
Saw the angel lose her wings.

I will hope for this.
Nothing else but this.

Open doorway.
Looking your way.
The breath before the plunge.

I have come to this.
Nothing else but this.
Drawn to what I miss.
Nothing else but this.

On the Inside

that night I told you to be careful
in the way I could not be careful myself.
you left the party and I walked from drink to drink
wishing the best for you, knowing it was the worst for me.

it is a horrible wonderful thing to be in love with you.
to get to hear you sing for hour after hour
but never be the subject of the song.
to listen and listen and listen.

I carry your equipment to gigs.
I am your ride home, your calendar.
I let you choose the radio station, the time.
and in return, yours is the only goodnight I ever need.

I've lost track of where friendship ends and falling begins.
(this is the foolish refrain of the hopelessly devoted.)
there are times I want to kiss you midsentence.
undo the not-doing with one gesture.

but I hesitate in the wondering.
she's taken the place that was never mine.
you and i have our sad misdirected love in common.
only yours sings out, while mine is a voice left on the inside.

I bide my time, pick at the petals, play the good best friend.
you ask me what I'm looking for, and I outline you.
you don't recognize the shape, offer other names.
you say my time will come, and I hope.

I know this is how the world works.
it would be funny, if it wasn't my heart.
she is the weakness you think of as strength.
while I am the strength you have no idea is there.

I am the one who knows who you are.
I want you to be happy.
and you could be
with me.

t w o

Tyler

Anton

Gail

Jill

My girlfriend is in love with Holden Caulfield

My girfriend is in love with Holden Caulfield
and it is driving me CRAZY. She has read that book
thirteen times, which is about eleven more times than
she's bothered to read me. Everything she sees now
is PHONY. Starbucks is PHONY. Our teachers are
PHONY. Society is PHONY. And love—well, love
is the phoniest of all. At first I tried real hard
to argue, but that made me one of THEM and not
HIM. She tells me he is sweet because he wants
to stop all of the little children from running off
a cliff. And I say can you possibly think of a situation
where a group of children would be running towards
a cliff? And she says I just DON'T GET IT. Which
is her way of saying she just doesn't get me, and how
I can get everything so wrong. Not like Holden,
who would be like seventy years old right now, but
is frozen at this age that I can't wait to leave. She says
she misses being a kid, just like Holden misses riding
the carousel. But what's going to stop us from getting on
the carousel, from sledding at midnight, from candy
and crushes? Just because we're having sex doesn't mean
we can't kiss. Holden is a failure with girls, and my girlfriend
says that's because he hasn't met the right girl, one who'd
UNDERSTAND him. She says this the same night we

60

argue for an hour about the fact that I always say "I love you"
before she does. I leave the room to sneak us some drinks
and when I get back she has THE BOOK out, read so often that
it's spineless. Whoever made the cover blank knew
what he was doing, because what image of Holden could be
stronger than the picture in my girlfriend's head?
We've been going out for five months now, sleeping
together for two, fighting over who loves who
for one. I used to love that she could love
a book so much. It was her first present to me.
I told her I loved it, when what I really meant was I loved
that it was from her. Then I made the mistake of
CRITICIZING. I said that Holden seemed pretty sad
and she said, yeah, that's because his brother died,
and I said it wasn't just that kind of sad. She said maybe
it took a certain kind of person to see the truth
in it, and because I loved her even then, I said she was
right. But the more I thought about it, the more I thought
less of it, and the more I thought less of it, the more she
thought less of me. And I began to think less of her
for thinking less of me. If I took up with hookers,
if I drank my daddy's money away, if I ridiculed everyone,
it wouldn't be charming. She wouldn't love that
in me. And, yes, Holden would keep those kids from
falling off the cliff, but WHO WOULDN'T? Does she think
I would just fold my arms or give them a pat on the back before they
sailed headfirst to the ground? We are all catchers, and it's sad
that she doesn't see it. Instead she sees the PHONINESS,
she deplores the world even after I point out that

I am in it. If she were running through the rye, if she
were headed toward that abyss, I would grab hold
with every ounce of my strength, with every scared beat
of my heart, with every thought that could only be for her.
And if I were to be running the same way, I'd like to think
she'd do the same. But maybe her hands would be busy
holding the book. Maybe she wouldn't see me, too intent
on looking for Phoebe from the carousel. Or waiting for Holden
to hold her, to wrap her in the pages of his arms,
to say she was the only one who truly knew him, as I
plunged past her, sad to be leaving, and a little
happy to be away.

suburban myths

there are alligators in the sewers of
Bloomfield Hills, and if you're coming home
late from a party—at, say, two in the morning—
you have to be careful because that's when
they lift the manhole covers and go to Blockbuster
to get videos to watch while they're underground
the next day. there was once a Blockbuster cashier
who tried to charge an alligator late fees
and they found his body the next morning
bitten in twenty-three different places. his blood
came out the faucets
                              for days.

teenagers are never joking. when seeking to prove
a point, principals and teachers should remember
that teenagers are never, ever sarcastic or ironic.
if they say, "I wish someone would drop a bomb
on this school right now," that means they have
arranged for a nuclear arsenal to be emptied
onto the school and should be immediately
suspended and ridiculed. if they say they were merely
coming up with a joking excuse to postpone a bio test,

reply that all jokes are funny, and that since dropping a bomb
on a school is not funny, it is therefore

not

a

joke.

there was this woman in Urbana who loved to eat
so much that it became her life. the neighbors stopped
seeing her. all they would see was a never-ending parade
of takeout deliverymen—pizza boys and Chinese box holders
and the girls from El Taco Grande who swore the woman
left more money for tips than anyone else. they never saw
her, though. this went on for years. she left twenties
under the front mat and bribed boys from McDonald's to take
their breaks delivering her cartons of supersize fries, supersize
sodas, supersize burgers. eventually, this one kid John
and his friends decided to break in and scare her.
but she got them instead, because they found her
dead in the kitchen, weighing nearly as much as the bed
she'd moved in there just so she could be close
to all the things
she loved.

everybody's heard the one about love being
easy. it happened once to this boy from Newton.
the girl he liked ended up being the girl who
liked him. when he saw her in the hall, she brightened
and spoke music to him. there was nothing
to be afraid of. even though he was white and
she was black, blessings rained down from
all of their friends and family and even a couple of
teachers. they never played games with each other,
they never had to worry where they stood, because
if either of them had a moment of wavering,
the other would say I love you and would mean it
and all doubts were forgiven because in this one case
it was found that love

                    conquers all.

all alike families are happy. there was this one
family in Sarasota that was even identical.
people couldn't tell who the father was,
the mother was, the son was. they were all so
happy that it didn't matter who they were.
eventually a circus bought them and charged
admission for people to see them in their
natural happy habitat. spectators would come
from all across the state to see them eat
dinner together, watch the same channels together,

talk to each other at length. People called them freaks
not because they were identical, but because they were
so

    damn

        happy.

popularity is in fact a democracy. it is a fair
and square contest. every month, students vote,
and the kindest, most compassionate people
are always chosen to be the most popular.
just as we always choose the best person
in the country to be president, we always pick
the most deserving people to be popular.
they, in turn, humbly accept and prove to be
role models for all the rest of the students,
because their position is so much based
on worth and not at all on

                        looks or

                              cruelty.

there was this girl from Springfield who was
asked to the prom by a guy who really, really
hated her. he did it on a dare, and the girl was

unaware of it. she used all her money to buy
a dress and a flower for his jacket. the dress
was as white as a cloud in a dream and the
flower was a red rose. she waited on prom night
for him to pick her up. instead he and his friends
drove by over and over while she waited on the curb,
holding the rose in her hand. her dress
billowed in the wind and sucked up all the dirt
from the tires as the boys called her a ferret
and honked so all the neighbors would see.
she couldn't take it and the next time they drove by
she jumped out in front. she went crashing through
the windshield and her dress fanned out in the
impact, suffocating them all. the rose

                                              was not

                                                    damaged.

the town of North Orange is still recovering
from the day the students came to biology class
and found their teacher lying on a table,
his chest cut open, his body dripping with
formaldehyde. the window was open and all
the frog tanks were

                        empty.

the kid in the back of the class opening fire
into his notebook, ink explosions of thought,
is the kid to watch out for, the kid who one day
will bring a gun to school and take revenge for
not being the person you are, the person you want
him to be. if he wears black, he's twice as likely,
if he wears headphones at lunch, he's three times
as likely. if you look over his shoulder, you will see
that everything he writes is
                            always
                                    about
                                         you.

Gospel

You've got to live the gospel.
I'm not talking practicing what you preach—
there is no *practicing* here.
I am talking *living* what you preach.
And to do that, you gotta preach what you live.
I know what I'm here for
and I know what the Lord is here for.
The gospel. I will live and die by the gospel.

I look around me and I see all the problems.
I know people aren't living the gospel.
I know they are too busy.
The world is too loud.
The sounds you hear in the hall are not
the substance of love and kindness.
I hear gossip, I hear spite, I hear fear.
I do not hear the gospel.
I do not feel the gospel.
Except inside me. I can feel it there.

And my friends.
There are not many of us, Lord knows.
But we are there for each other.
The Lord loves things in three, and we are three.
Lanie with her blue-covered Bible,

Tracy with her red-covered Bible,
and me with what I call the Original Black.
It's not that we walk around all buttoned up,
not a part of the world. Don't think that.
We know what's happening, and what's what.
But we also know which end is up.

I have never heard a more beautiful word than
Hallelujah!
When I was a little girl, I looked forward to Sunday.
I would have my dress out by Friday,
my shoes lined up underneath like my legs were already in them.
I would count the ladies in the choir and feel like I was waiting
my turn, practicing my voice for their kind of calling.
As I grew older, I got worried—I learned that, at least in my church,
choir ladies never die. I thought there'd be no opening for me
and felt like the worst sinner for wanting a space so bad.
But when my time came, old Mrs. Hayes decided she'd rather listen,
so I moved on up there and found my songs.
Hallelujah!

School is not like church.
I know a lot of people in my school are happy about this,
but I think that's because they've known the wrong kind
of churches, the ones that hold back instead of lifting up.
I've seen the inside of some of those churches.
Let me tell you, the gospel isn't there.
Like turning on the television and hearing some man
(calls himself a preacher!)

use his cross to hit people over their heads,
spewing all that hate in the name of the Lord.
That is *not* the gospel.
That is *not* why we are here.

I would like school to be like church.
I would like it to be a place where we sing to the rafters.
I would like our lives to be *illuminated*.

I will admit this:
Lanie, Tracy, and I do not speak up as often as we should.
We will get home full of other people's shame—
Did you see how Jimmy made Maria cry in class?
Did you see how Mr. Thomas yelled at Max for not agreeing?
Did you see how lonely that girl looked at lunch?
What we are saying is that we *did* see.
And what did we do?
We acted blind, and we moved on.
That is not the gospel.

Lanie, Tracy, and I sit in the front of the class.
It is too easy to be ignored in this world,
so you've gotta put yourself up front
if you want to be counted, and to count.
Even if we're not always being *illuminated*,
we're being given tools to build a house
of the gospel, to make sure our lives are strong.
Lanie's mama never made it this far;
she left school to have Lanie.

If she could do it all again, I know
she wouldn't be sitting in the back.

The boys, however, fight over the back.
Trying to separate themselves,
make their own slouching kingdom.
The ruder the boy, the farther back he sits.
As if that justifies the way he talks too loud.
Thinking so much of himself that he can be
in the back and still be the center of it all.
I have nothing to say to boys like that,
and the things they have to say to me
are nothing I will repeat, not even to myself.
I let their scorn wash over me like water.

But not all of the boys in the back are like this.
There is another, the quiet one watching.
Writing in his notebook like he's composing
his own scripture, making himself something
to believe. I know his name is Anton,
only because our teacher likes to call on him
when he is most far away. Our teacher
is mean like that—he wants to play favorites,
but Lord knows he doesn't like any of us.

That day.
Even though my back is turned,
I can see what's going on.
The sound of their taunting—

I know what that looks like.
Words like *freak* and *loser*—
I know what kind of face says them.
Our teacher is ignoring it;
he does not have the strength to deal with it.
Or maybe he agrees with what's being said.
He agrees by talking math as the notebook
is pulled out of Anton's hand.
Even though he sees what's going on,
his back is turned.

I hear Anton pulling against them.
And I know what will happen next.
He does not let go; they tear
it out of his hands.
And then the ripping sounds.
The teacher keeps talking.
One rip after another.
The laughter of the boys.
These boys, who will not go near a book,
begin to read out loud in spiteful voices,
making a mockery of words.
there are alligators in the sewers.
when he saw her in the hall, she brightened
and spoke music to him.
found their teacher lying on a table,
his chest cut open.
That laughter that is not joyous at all.
It is fueled by misery—

someone else's misery.
There is a blast of music, and that is when
I turn around. Anton has put on his headphones.
He is blocking it out. One boy dangles a page
in front of his eyes. He doesn't reach for it.
He closes his eyes.

I have had enough.
That is the only way I can explain it.
As if the Lord himself writes that sentence
across my mind's eye:
I have had enough.
He is turning the music louder and louder
so we can all hear it, even if it can't
drown out the taunting.
The teacher tells him to *turn that music off*
and that is it.
Enough.

I rise from my seat and point at
those boys in the back.
I take all the air of the gospel into my lungs
and I shout out
How dare you?
I call out
Do unto others.
I yell
You should be ashamed.
I testify to that.

All it takes is one person to speak up.
Sometimes that's not enough,
but in this case it is.
Other kids—Lanie, Tracy,
other girls, a few boys
join the choir, saying
lay off and *stop it* and
give it back to him.
Anton with his eyes open now,
his ears still covered in noise.
Looking at me
with a mix of surprise and sadness.
Mostly his eyes are dead.

The teacher steps in now and says—
I swear, the man is a fool or worse—
What's going on here? What happened?
And I am now weaker than I aspire to be,
because I do not tell him all that he allowed,
I do not point to the causes and the effects.
These are not questions meant to be answered,
anyway—like all of his questions
that don't involve his mathematics.
He tells the boys to hand back the notebook,
and they present Anton with the pieces,
as if that is some punch line to the joke.

I sit down, and as I do, I think:

Lord, give me the strength to fight unkindness.
I will not abide it. I will not abide.

The bell rings, ending class
and nothing else. One boy pushes the pages over
as he leaves, scattering them on the floor.
I walk back and help Anton re-gather them.
He mumbles thanks and looks away.
And I resolve then and there:
I will be good to this boy.
I tell him he is welcome
and leave before he has to feel like
he must say something else.

It used to be that when Lanie, Tracy, and I
walked in the hallways, we were all there was to it.
We only noticed one another in all that commotion.
I probably passed Anton a thousand times in those halls,
but it's only after that math class that I realize he's there.
I am talking to Lanie two periods later, my heart finally
calming down from what happened, and as we're going
to the library, I stop seeing her and I see him walking
toward me. Headphones on, head-to-toe black clothes.
He is in his own world, and while that world is very private,
it's also not very big. When his looking comes to me,
I raise my hand and he nods back. Our recognition.
He is there again when the next period is over.
Our paths have been made to cross from different directions.

The next morning I add a *hello*.
He responds with a *hello*.
We walk into math class together
and he sits next to me, in the front.
That afternoon, I smile with my *hello*.
He does not smile back, but he does
switch off his headphones.

Lanie and Tracy are amused
in a not-completely-amused way.
They do not ask me about it in school,
but that Sunday after church, they have a litany
of questions about what's going on.
They call him my Dressed in Darkness Boy
and tell me that when I turned down Curtis Stone
after he wanted to take me for a drive,
they had no idea that I was looking for this instead.
I tell them to have a little faith in me.
The Lord is not the only one
who moves in mysterious ways.

Yes, he is dressed in darkness.
But my eyes are getting used to the dark.
I notice the tree of black ink
he's drawn on his black bag.
There is a moment in math class when I knock
my pencil off my desk and we both bend
to get it. His hair does not smell of darkness.
There are flowers underneath the ground.

We begin to speak
after class. Two minutes of talking
about nothing before he retreats.
Lanie and Tracy say maybe he's not
used to talking to other people.
The boys in the back jeer at us
when they walk past, but Anton and I
withstand that, try to talk over their noise.
Secretly I wonder if we'll ever have
more than these two minutes.
Then Anton surprises me and asks me
if I want to come over sometime.
I ask him where, and he says his house.
I'm not sure about that, so I ask him
if he'd want to come to church first.
In some part of my brain, this makes sense.
He says he will, that Sunday.

Now Lanie and Tracy are sure
I'm insane. But I tell them this.
I tell them to consider blessings.
The thing about blessings is that
they aren't just delivered to you.
There is some mystery to their appearance,
but once they're in your reach,
you have to do something for them.
They ask me if Anton
is my blessing or if I am his.
I say that neither of us is a blessing,

but that both of us could be, everything
around us could be. The boys in the back
of the room could be a blessing if they push us
to a kindness they would never
understand, but that we can begin
to understand.

Lanie and Tracy point out
that I will be sitting in the choir
when Anton comes to our church.
They will be the ones he will
sit between. I tell them they too
are certainly part of the blessing.
And when Sunday comes, they are
waiting for me out front. Our families
are used to us separating ourselves from them,
sitting in our own pew. Anton arrives
only a few minutes later. His darkness
has reshaped itself into a black shirt,
a black tie, a black jacket. Black pants
and the same black shoes. He takes off
his headphones as he gets closer.
He smiles.

I have never brought someone into my
church before. Nobody but cousins and aunts,
friends of my parents and their children,
the ones I never liked as much as I was
supposed to. This visitor is different.

The choir ladies look at me with curiosity
and some disapproval as we put on our robes.
Honey, Myrna Walker asks,
who is that boy? And I'm glad
she's come right out and asked, because
I can say *He's a friend* and let that explain
as much as can be explained. Myrna nods
as the organ begins to play. That is our cue.

When I sing the Lord's words,
I am usually looking at the Lord.
Not seeing him as you'd see a picture,
but letting my feeling of the gospel
block out everything else.
Hallelujah!
I am elevated higher than my life
can usually go. I am filled with all the joys
and troubles and wisdoms and challenges
of the world, and I sing them out of me
as the psalms preach it,
as the preacher leads it,
as the Lord sings it in all our voices
and in the music of the organ and the
shaking, agreeing bodies that chime in from
the congregation.

This time I look down as I'm singing.
I know exactly where Lanie and Tracy will sit,
so I look right over to see him.
And at first I feel the urge to laugh,
because he is so clearly over his head with us.
He thinks there's a certain way
his body should move, a certain place
his hands should be. When the truth is that
we just move our bodies wherever our bodies
want to take us. I sing louder
and he looks right at me, finally
getting it, because what I am saying
with the rise of my voice is that I know
he understands what music is about,
he has seen the Lord in it, even if it's not
my Lord. He begins to sway along,
loses himself a little to something
greater. I will admit right here he looks
ridiculous, white boy in black clothing.
But there is also something beautiful
in his trying.

I believe
in glory, in praise.
I could not sing
if I did not believe.
My singing
is how I come closer
to glory, to praise.

By singing
I keep such faith alive.
I become part of the redeemer
by singing redemption.
I become part of the rock
by singing its weight.
I become part of the gospel
by voicing it.

Listen to us.
We believe.

After the service is over,
after the congregation becomes
a collection of people once more,
I take off my robe and return
to Lanie and Tracy and Anton.
I ask Anton what he thought
and he thanks me for bringing him,
for showing him my church.
My parents come over, itching
for an introduction. Anton falls quiet
but stays respectful as my father
measures him in a handshake
and my mother asks after his parents.
Even though I do not like to lie
in church, I tell my parents
the four of us are going out
after. My mother says *That's*

nice while my father stays quiet.
Our preacher comes over, sweat
still on his brow, his voice still
at a preaching volume. He welcomes
Anton and says he hopes he'll come back.
Anton says he hopes to do so,
and I can see the preacher approving,
even if he's more than a little confused.

Lanie and Tracy walk a little of the way
with us. Usually we'd be chattering
about what people wore to church or
which husbands and wives didn't sit
as close as they usually did. But Anton
alters our conversation, so we find ourselves
in an unusual silence. Anton recognizes this
and starts to ask us church questions.
We tell him how long Myrna Walker's
been in the choir, how many people
usually come to services, how the gospel
is something that's there all your life,
so it's not something you really know
you're learning until you've learned it.
Lanie asks him where his family goes
to church, and he says that the place
they avoid is St. Elizabeth's. They go
to Christmas Mass as if it's a show
every year.

There isn't any signal,
but Lanie and Tracy know when it's time
to leave. They'll go home, change out of
their dresses and into homework clothes.
They thank Anton nicely for coming,
and he thanks them for putting up with him.
I try to imagine us doing this every Sunday,
and I can't picture it really.
But for today it is working in this
awkward kind of working. And that
is enough for a beginning.

I don't know where I thought he'd live,
but it's a big house on a street graced
with trees and long driveways.
I am telling him about the choir,
about all the people in it, and while
I'm the one talking, I can feel him
falling silent, losing words. When he says
We're here, he is apologizing for something
I don't know yet. As soon as we walk through
the back door, he starts darting through
the house. I can hear the television on
in the other room, people watching golf,
but instead of making introductions
Anton runs me up the stairs to his room,
then closes the door with emphasis.
Not to keep me in, but to keep
everyone else out.

I am overwhelmed
by his room. The walls are all covered
with posters and stickers for bands
I have never heard of, have never heard.
Anton heads straight to his stereo
and unleashes a blast. I cannot believe
the noise. Surely if Job had a sound
forced in his ears, it would be this.
It's an angry screaming with a dark
something underneath. *Do you
like it?* Anton yells to me, sitting down
on the edge of his bed. He is so proud
of it. He is sharing his music with me,
and who am I to say that it is Job's music,
that it is music like an assault? His chair
is covered with books and his jacket,
so I sit on the floor by the bed. The song
changes, the disc switches, but it's more
of the same. He drums the air, asks me
if I can feel the bass. And I do feel it,
working into my body from where
my hands touch the floor.

I don't know what to say.
I look at the posters, see that there are
some drawings on the walls, too.
The disc changes again, and suddenly
it's Billie Holiday singing about stormy
weather, it just keeps raining all the time.

At the same moment, I see a drawing of
Billie on the wall, small and sad.
Anton slides down on the floor next to me
and before I know it, his hand is gently
on mine. I turn to him and see how
nervous he is. I notice he hasn't taken off
his tie, he is still dressing up nice for me.
I am about to say something when he
removes his hand from mine and reaches
the other hand around, touching my cheek
then my shoulder. He says my name
like it is the gospel itself, and then he
moves his lips onto mine. He holds me
and it's that drowning kind of holding.
It is all so fast. He pulls back to look at me
and I don't have to say anything. He loses
his courage, he loses his footing. The
song shifts back to noise and he starts
telling me he is sorry, so sorry, and he
is so flustered and so lost and Lord, I am
lost too, as he stammers and begins to cry
because he is so lost. And the only thing
I can think to do is find him, pull him
back to me, that drowning kind of holding
again, but with the feeling that we won't
drown, not today. And he is crying he is
sorry and I am telling him there's no reason
to be sorry. With one hand I keep him
to me and with the other hand I turn down

the noise in time to hear him say
he loves me.

I have never been given these words
in this way before. This small piece of
gospel, three parts hosanna, two parts
testimony, one part lamentation.
He is apologizing again, this time
for loving me, and I am still holding him
so gently that our bodies could be spirits.
And I find that I am loving him, too,
and that I am sorry, too, because I love him
in the way that the gospel can love;
I love him in the way I want to love
everybody, not in the way that would make me
kiss him back in the way he might want to be
kissed. I am sure he is confusing
these kinds of love, that what he wants
from me is caring, not a roll around
on the floor. Or maybe that's just
what I think.

He lets go before I do.
I see him eye the stereo, wanting
to turn it up again. But he doesn't.
Instead he says he's sorry again,
and I tell him to stop. I tell him
everything is right by me. I ask him
to put Billie Holiday back on.

She is not a gospel singer.
She sings like someone who tried
to live by the gospel, but was hurt
at every chance there was.

I barely know the words
but I start singing along anyway.
I try to make it into the gospel,
and when that doesn't work, I just
sing it from a different place.
Eventually Anton turns the stereo
down and sits there carefully,
looking at me. I close my eyes and
raise the roof for him. I sing so loud
that the stormy weather will cease,
that the television will turn off,
that the black clothes will unveil
all the color that we are underneath.
I sing to be a blessing, and I sing
because the song is a blessing to me.
The song goes: *I got the whole world
in my hands, the whole world in
my hands.* You've gotta live the gospel,
you've gotta take the whole world in
your hands and show it kindness.
Is love the gospel, or is the gospel
love? Only the Lord knows, and the Lord
isn't saying. It's up to the rest of us
to make it out. To make it work.

When I am done,
when the song is over and we are left
in that silence that can be so many things,
Anton looks at me with such an open heart
that I know mine will open to him, and
that we will have that, which is
everything.

As the last echo of the song
leaves the room, he applauds
for a moment, smiles at me,
loosens his tie, and says
Amen.

lying awake beside you, these thoughts run through my head

the inhale, the exhale.
the watching in the dark.

you can sleep through anything,
except your parents coming home.

but they are gone for the weekend,
so I am here.

watching as you sleep.
the gentle movements.

the blue room.
you have no idea.

you sleep, I watch.
the afterwards.

we have just been as close as two people can be.
you have said those three words.

and I believed it.
now you are asleep,

and it is dark,
and I am back with myself again.

you have no idea.
this dark.

it would be so easy to let you take me with you.
that waking dreamland we escape to every now and then.

to be the person you think I am.
that person worthy of your love.

but I'm not.
I do not deserve you.

your breath,
my confession.

I have hurt people.
different people, the same hurt.

I have done things because I wanted to.
for no other reason than wanting to.

I have done things.
I have been that darkness.

you are sleeping with your arm around the pillow,
your feet dangling off the bed.

there should only be one of us here.
you have no idea that I will break your heart.

when you break someone's heart,
you also break your own.

whenever I approach the truth,
you back away from it.

you don't want to know.
but you should know.

the more you love me, the more I will ruin you.
I will take my darkness and I will push it inside you.

lying awake beside you,
these thoughts go through my head.

I have done unforgivable things.
(you inhale, you exhale)

I have taken advantage of other people's weaknesses in order to
    cover my own.
I have slept with boys even though I knew they would later make
    me want to die.

I have lied so often that I've lost all track of the truth.
I have stolen people's boyfriends, because I knew I could.

and then I dumped them like everyone else.
because there was always someone else.

I have never been faithful.
until you.

but I do not know if that can last, if I can overcome who I am.
you open your arms to me and I want to tell you not to.

do not expose yourself to me.
the last boy who did that ended up shattered.

he could not stop asking me *why?*
he told me he loved me and I slapped him.

he thought I was playing, but I wasn't.
I am that damaged.

you sleep so innocently, and I watch so guiltily.
I didn't think it would come to this.

you kissed me at a party.
we both wanted to.

we hooked up—something that sounds like two metal pieces
    fastening together.
one holding the other, although it's often hard to tell which is
    which.

I liked your eyes and I could tell you liked my body.
I was fine with that, because it was not supposed to lead to this.

because I do care,
enough that I should leave you.

I am not capable of something you are capable of.
that is, love.

I have the capacity for attraction.
even for admiration.

you deserve someone who will turn her world for you,
someone who will give you sweetness.

I am unkind.
I am that kind.

you say you do not see it.
you say I am too hard on myself.

but I have lived with myself for too many years.
I know exactly how hard I am.

you will argue with me.
(not now, you are asleep)

you will rip yourself to shreds to prove that I am worth loving.
you will not hear the chorus of everyone I've let down.

they sing from inside me,
sing from the darkness.

you do not know them.
they are from another town, another time.

but from the same person who now lies here next to you,
who can run her hand over your shoulder and make you shiver.

pull up the sheet.
inhale, exhale.

you are so beautiful.
this light.

the night I gave up on myself was not long ago.
right before I met you.

I was the new girl, and wanted that.
to make me a new person. redraw myself.

I was pretty enough for Cara to take me into her group.
I was phony enough to let her think I was grateful.

we shopped, we gossiped, we made plans.
I let her confide, and let her think I was confiding.

her birthday.
it was her birthday.

she hadn't been going out with Roger for long.
she loved loving him, and I knew that.

I didn't really like him.
let me say that outright—I didn't really like him.

we were at her house, drinking her parents' liquor.
I was bored; she kept asking how I was.

we had spent an hour figuring out what she would wear.
that is, what Roger would like.

I knew Roger didn't care.
he wasn't the kind to notice what his girlfriend was wearing.

other girls, though.
me, for instance.

I was not drunk.
Roger was.

right in front of Cara.
because it was simple.

there is doing wrong without knowing you are doing it.
that can be somehow excused, at least over time.

but I knew it was wrong,
and I did it anyway.

because I liked the power it gave me.
because I liked being able to do it.

I could not be a new girl.
I took him to the backyard.

and the darkness there was not like this darkness.
it was a pitch-black emptiness.

there was no pleasure in it.
just bored destruction.

Cara never forgave me.
I was glad for that.

to have a reason to feel this way about myself.
I gave myself the reason.

you weren't there that night.
I would have to wait another month to meet you.

but you must have heard.
you must have been warned.

I am a damager.
and yet, you hold me.

I am so tired of the phoniness,
especially my own.

with you I feel real.
but then I worry about the me that lies beneath.

at the end of the book, Holden says don't tell anybody anything.
I say all these things without ever saying them out loud.

this is the voice I hear.
I always hear.

the inhale, the exhale.
you are so soft like this, touchable.

breath is not aware of its history; it is just breath.
I wish I could be like that, or love could be like that.

you give me hope.
I debate whether I deserve it.

the rise, the fall, the rise.
if I hold you, you will know it in your dreams.

I run to the cliff, and then see you sleeping.
I stop.

this darkness is so many things.
it is my past in my present.

forgive me for what I might do to you.
the threat of my past in my future.

the inhale, the exhale.
the unsilent silence.

the blue room.
seeing in the dark.

the unearned comfort of you.
my regrets.

I regret
I will try.

three

Anne

Jamie

Pete

Clara

Fragments

1. Reliquary

The slide is offered to the darkness,
gold and jewels in the shape of a child.
"She was a young girl in the tenth century"—
nothing else is known.

How sad it must be for you
to be nothing more than a hollow statue,
to have your tomb preserved
and your story forgotten.

2. Hourglass

I often want to pour more sand
into the hourglass; you know the shape,
how it is supposed to mean time.
We are caught in the narrow middle.

You and I play games with each other.
I turn over the hourglass and you protest.
You are not ready to move yet. So instead
you knock it over, grab my hand.

3. Anne Frank

When I was twelve, I decided to be Anne Frank
for Halloween. She was my favorite author,
the person I wanted to be when I grew up.
The neighbors didn't know what to do

when I showed up in my schoolgirl outfit,
the red plaid diary under my arm. Danny was with me,
dressed as Charlie Chaplin. I guess that was my fantasy,
to imagine them walking down our street together.

4. Diary

I catch you reading my diary; you argue
if I hadn't wanted you to read it,
I wouldn't have left it out.
If only I'd left you out, too.

You say you only read one page,
the one where I rant against war.
I take the diary back and write a new page,
so you can read my disappointment in you.

5. Quilt

My great-grandmother made it for my grandmother
and her marriage bed. From there, it ended up
with me. It is a crazy quilt, colors crashing
every which way. I've studied it for hours,

trying to find a pattern beneath it all. I asked
my mother about it, and she said that some things
are just random. Then she cried for my grandmother,
and I went back to find the beauty in the random.

6. Present

Just when I decide to leave you, you make me
a card. There is no occasion attached,
just a kaleidoscope collage of the world,
green mountains, blue oceans, the sun.

You've used tape, not glue, and the edges
are already starting to split. Inside you've written
This is all for you, and I'm amazed
you've given me something I will always keep.

7. Sappho

She leaves me fragments and they are more real
than a library of novels. Wisps of words
from centuries ago, caught in the translation.
I often feel I am living in fragments, skipping

over words, leaving the rest of the sentence
blank in order to move on to the next page.
Maybe there is hope in fragments, that what is lost
can always be filled in by someone who knows.

8. This Moment

You drive me down to the shore
and I push you right into the waves.
You laugh and pull me in with you.
I feel the shells beneath my feet.

We hold each other at the same time,
the sun dancing in your hair.
And I think, this is what's eternal.
Not for us, but in itself.

the day

a banner of light breaks into the room, five minutes before
  the alarm awakes
a cold when the blankets are removed
a concern that passes
a detail unnoticed by the next moment

a look at the clock
a memory of saying hello to an angel in a dream

a squint when the lightbulb switches on
a stop as the water turns warm, then hot
afraid of the day in inarticulate ways
after the shower, the half dream will wash away
as incomplete as the ghost who still reaches for
  doorknobs

as I choose which clothes to wear
as I pack the bag for the day
asking for nothing in return

assignments, astrology, asymmetry
at breakfast, zack eats pancakes three at a time
attempting to be a good sibling, I ask about anne
awestruck by love, or something like it, he answers with
  an unaccustomed sweetness

back to the routine
before the radio is turned off
before the ride is over
begin right here

beginning to understand where hesitations come from
betrayal is in the air, my thoughts
better to not have to choose between safe and sorry

biology is no way to start the day
blackboards are never black anymore
blameless, jakob slips me a note that says *she's being
   ridiculous*
borderline between sides
but we used to be friends

can't be that simple
capillaries are invisible to the eye
catalog all the reasons a friendship ends
caught between those reasons is the truth I'll never know

certain there will never be certainties
circle the following option
circulation is what keeps us alive

clamoring in the halls
clutching to the hope of not seeing her, not being called out
come here
come over

contradict me again and I will break your heart

curvaceous ms. gunderson presides over history
daniel asks me if I'm doing okay
daring me to explode
deceptively, I smile

despite all the thoughts that run through your head, you're
    never really ready to let go, are you?
distract me with the prussian war, ms. gunderson
distract me with the way you brush back your bangs
do whatever you have to do, I said to tegan

drown in the word ANYTHING written on a desk
duration is a relative thing

early warnings are never heeded
easy to say now that I should've known
end that line of speculation; go to gym

even though we never made this walk together
even though we weren't that kind of pair
even when I promised not to do this
everything is missing right now

fashion your composure
feel normal in your gym clothes
field that birdie like such things matter

for another lover—no
for freedom—not really
for hundreds of minor infractions—perhaps
for seven months, we were together
for the time being, there's no way to know the reasons

forget, forgone, forgotten
fourteen things of hers are still in my locker

gail is humming a hymn as she walks with her trinity into
    math class
gentleness is a statement
gestures are everything we need

give it time, tegan said to me last night, as if a breakup was
    something you could leave out to dry
go, I shouted, but what I meant was the opposite

graph the coordinates, find the parabola
group it all onto the page, even though it goes on forever
growing up is hard to do

had I seen the distance?
had I seen the distance, could I have crossed it?
halved, harmed, hard to say
having enough had been enough

her

here is the place we'd meet for two minutes before the next
    bell
here is the time we were the only ones left in the school
    and kissed by the light of the exit sign
here is where we
here is where we're not

hidden in the library for study hall, I try to think
    compositionally for my english homework
hip to my distress, jed comes over to listen to
    whatever I have to say
his concern is as clear as my confusion
his pen doodles in my margin as I tell him
history often comes sooner than you think

honestly, she said before saying it was over
honing in on my every vulnerability, my every fear
hopefully, I tried to persuade her
hopelessly, I tried to persuade her

hours cannot measure what I feel
housed inside me like a caged tiger
how strange it feels to talk about it
how was I planning to get through this alone?

I do not cry
I have had enough of that
I speak these words as a way of controlling them

instead of telling me everything is okay
instead of wallowing and saying life sucks
instinctively jed lets me release my story
it is a way of releasing myself

it's nearly time to go to lunch
it's tempting to skip it
jed asks me if I'm coming, ready to be the company
   I keep
jitters crescendo, but I close my blank homework
   and try to prepare for the worst

jocks crowd the lunch line
joking loudly
jostling my tray

jungle laws apply here
just as I think I can do it, I see her at a new table
jutting her attention into a fake conversation
juvenile in her avoidance

karen and daniel and sam are sitting at our usual table,
   and I know the choice couldn't have been an easy one
keeping my eye on her, I try to restore some faith
kidding myself that this victory wins the war
kindness is clearly not the point
kiss me one last time is the sentence I will remember

label me any way you want
lace your disdain through every thought in this room
ladder your reasons until they reach the sky
lament as loud as you can—I know you're thinking of me

landing right beside me at the table, jed shifts the conversation
   to lighter things
lantern lines of words to help guide me away from her

last night I couldn't imagine this new reality
late into the night I pictured it all falling apart

laugh despite her
laugh to spite her
lean forward, listen to your friends
leap if you have to
learn that things will mend in a new way

leaving my guard down has always been second nature to me
lecturing myself to avoid looking over at her
led by curiosity, or desire, or sheer stupidity, I turn and lose

left like there is no such thing as memory

legs soon crowd between us
lending me his english essay, jed tells me to copy quick
letting me twist his words my own way
letting me work through the last minutes of her avoidance

like we never even

listening to my friends' last assurances before the last bell rings
little booster shots of self-esteem
little prognostications of a better future
little protests that she could be so unfair, so wrong

locating mr. feldman in the clutter of his art room, I warn him
    I will not be sculpting any goddesses today
locking me in his stare, he warns me to paint neither red nor blue
lone among my teachers, I think he understands

looking through the resins and the pigments, I feel my senses'
    slow return
looping circles into patterns
loosening the muscles that have been so sympathetic to my hurt
losing the fear of touch
losing the knowledge that I touched her, and look what happened

loss takes as much as love does, sometimes more
low voices still say it was my fault
lures of truth turn out to be hooks

making circles
making lines
making meaningless meaning
making signs not meant to be read

many minutes pass, until mr. feldman breaks my spell by breaking
   the news that the period is over
mapping my design with his finger, he tells me I am blessed
marvelous words in an offhand tone
maybe that's all I need

me gusta no español, but I have to go to class anyway
measuring my words too carefully, I make it through an oral quiz

memories return to me in the pause that follows.
merely two seats away, mary and pete wear necklaces they made
   for each other.
messy, this collection of recollections
midway through a sentence, she would chew her necklace,
    and I would always buy her new beads
mine remains on my neck—it hadn't occurred to me to take it off

miserable, misguided, misled
missing her is not an option right now
missing her seems to be a given

mr. randall is in a bad mood for English
my salvation is jed, who sends an endless stream of notes my way
never mentioning her by name, only as The Evil One
newfound bitterness, humor in the hating—
no, not hating

notice how fickle feelings can be
now I'm better, now I'm worse

nowhere is it written how to deal with this

only thirty more minutes
over and over until it is over

papers are handed in
people look at me and I know they have heard
perhaps they've heard her version
pestering, pitiful, played out, possessive
possibly they don't believe her

preparing to leave, jed proposes an ice-cream-from-container
    afternoon
probably I should take him up on it, but more than anything,
    I want sleep
professing my true exhaustion, I tell him I'll be okay
profoundly sick at heart, but okay

purposefully, I avoid the hallway where her locker resides
pushing my gaze straight to the floor, I try to navigate until I
    must look up
putting myself right in her path, right in her line of sight
puzzled by what to do

racing heart stops me
raising my eyes to meet hers . . .
reacting as she looks right past me . . .
realizing she is going to pretend I am not here

reaping, rebuffing, redrawing, reflecting, regarding, regressing,
rehearsing, reiterating, reliving, remembering, reopening, repaying,
repealing, replying, retracing, retreating, returning, revoking

right at this moment, I cannot imagine it being any worse
right here, I have been turned into nothing
right now, I am negated

right or wrong, I am pummeled by her theatrics
riven to the spot, unable to call her on it
robbed even of that

roller coasters run smoother than my mind
rope couldn't pull me home faster
row row row your boat, even as it sinks
rude entertainment for everyone in the hall to see

run to your locker
run to your nearest friend and get a ride
rush through the conversation and try not to cry

safe in my room
searching that moment for the motivation I need
see, she is not worth it
see, she never loved you
see, there is no going back

seesaw through the haze
sing out all the doubts you ever had

singe the memories, because they are the things that get lost in the fire

sitting on the edge of my bed
skipping to the ending
slaying the tiger even as it claws
sleep calling me
slowly, I give in to it

somehow the knocking wakes me, hours later
someone calling me to get ready for dinner
something angry in her voice

spare me one more fault, one more argument
speak to me later, I plead silently
special dispensation for the dumped
spoken too soon

starting with my lateness, moving on to my afternoon
    nap and the paint left on the dining room table
stepmother and I have been through this so many times
stifling my yell takes all of my strength

stupidly, zack comes in late, too, and gets his share of
    the earful
substituting apologies for defiance, he brushes her off and
    looks at me carefully
suddenly I realize he hadn't heard until this afternoon
suffering on my behalf, he draws her wrath away from me

table conversation is cordial and strained
taking food to stop my hunger is pointless
tastes feel strange in my mouth

teach me how to see this years from now
tear out the last seams

tegan

the answer is to just let go
the betrayal is to the past
the cocoon dangles empty
the desire outlasts the object
the effort lingers
the frustration is in how pointless the effort was
the ghost does not make itself transparent
the heart knows nothing except its own mind
the ideas are not enough
the jealousy is always there
the killing blow is sometimes the softest
the life you lead can be detoured
the moment you know cannot be taken back
the new you will try to bury the old me
the opportunity has passed
the past is inopportune
the questions all grow from why
the reality will always be contended
the sadness will ebb
the trouble is the time it might take

the ugly words cannot be erased, only discredited
the versions are never the same
the wonder is that we make it through
the x is the unknown variable
the yesterday cannot be repeated
the zenith is the point when you look down and realize you're
   no longer below

there is no use in staying at the table
thoughts can follow you anywhere
turning the tv off, I head back to my room
tv only seems garish, fake

under the covers, under the watch of my glow-in-the-dark stars
up until this moment, I have held back from the edge
veering away from the flashing-before-my-eyes
votive darkness, though, draws the memories to me

wading in, because I know I have to

we ate raspberries from each other's hands
we carved our initials in benches, surrounded by a shape of our
   own invention
we danced around her bedroom without caring how we looked
we danced around so many subjects; if I brought up love, she usually
   brought it down
we fell into each other's arms as soon as no one else was in sight
we gave nothing that was irreplaceable, except time
we lit candles for each other when we were in different cities

we made fun of people together, to feel better about ourselves
we obsessed over the difference between what we meant and what we
    said
we ran out of things to say and watched videos instead
we screamed over what movie to see, being five minutes late
we were never honest with each other, not really

what's gone is gone

when the night grows so quiet you could hear the moon rise, zack
    comes to my door
whispering into the darkness
with careful steps entering
withdrawing my solitude
witnessing my arms crossed over my heart
x marks the spot

years between us, but not that many
years we've gone without this kind of conversation
yesterday he couldn't even tell something was wrong
yet here he is, now

you know, he says, *you'll get through this*
you live each day one at a time
you live every day all at once
you live with the possibility of good-bye
you move on.

you ponder in this darkness and see you're not alone

you realize you never felt alone
you subtracted one from your life, that's all

your heart is not as broken as you think, he says
you're not as dumb as you look, I reply

zack tells me it won't be as hard tomorrow, and I know he's right
zero hour has passed

Strong

We are all bodies, so I figured I wanted to be a strong one.
Without your body, you are nothing. You aren't even an idea.
I took off my shirt and people told me I was *well-defined*.

People respected the time I put in, all of the lifting,
the sweating, the pushing, the running, the exertion.
It was a discipline. My body was a discipline.

I wasn't always like that. None of us were.
The boy with the sunken chest gave himself over to me.
He wanted to be strong, because in this world you have to be.

It started with a blue barbell, something my mother had for aerobics.
I sat there in front of the television and lifted and lifted.
My father saw and got me ten pounds, fifty pounds, a bench.

I wanted Daniel, my neighbor, to lift with me. But he wasn't into it.
So I found my way to football, to wrestling, to the weight room.
I found the guys who knew what I meant, what I meant to be.

They said I would feel more in control. And I did.
They said I'd have to devote myself. And I did.
They said girls would look at me. And, damn, they did.

This body worked like a key. It got me into parties.
It got me the nod. It got me the smile and the tease. I was no fool.
Guys saw me, they saw power. Girls saw me, they saw sex.

Well, some of them. Daniel saw me and thought I was stupid.
Coach saw me and thought I could do more, strengthen.
And Mary . . . well, at first I didn't think Mary saw me at all.

Even though I'd never really talked to her, she got under my skin.
She wasn't in the group of girls that hung with my group of guys.
She was just this girl in Spanish class who was worse at it than I was.

When Señora Tilghman called on her, she never had the answer.
She never even knew what the question was, even if it was in English.
She wasn't just lost in space. She was space itself. Waiting to disappear.

She was not my type. My type was the kind of girl who'd go for me.
But there I was, fascinated by a girl who was nearly invisible.
As I was to her, like the crowd blurring when you're in the game.

With the football season on, I had to push my body beyond.
I wasn't like John, who'd drink eight Buds and still own the field.
I wasn't like Martin, such a natural that running fast is like breathing.

No, I had to watch myself. One false move and I'd find myself on JV.
The guys liked me and considered me part of the team. But no illusions.
If I held them back—if I didn't do my part—it was good-bye.

She was the one distraction I allowed myself. John laughed.
He said I could do better, which meant he didn't think she was hot.
He said I could probably circle her waist with my two hands.

I was amazed by her slightness, by the bones of her pale arms.
She was so breakable. I wondered: If I lifted her, would it feel like a wing?
I couldn't believe I was thinking such things. I wanted to know.

We went for weeks without speaking, with only me realizing we weren't.
Then one day I saw these silent tears falling from her eyes.
She was so thin and sad that her whole body looked like a line of tears.

There, in Spanish class. We were conjugating *conocer*, to know.
I reached into my pocket for a tissue, but all I had was a napkin.
I hesitated, then handed it over. She wiped her eyes before taking it.

She mouthed the words *thank you* to me. She stopped crying.
Composed, like nothing had happened. *Conozco. Conoces. Conoce.*
I watched as she rolled the napkin into a tiny rope around her finger.

She was so light, but her emotions were heavy. John said to run away.
But I walked toward her instead. Asked her out. Got her to talk a little.
Told her she was beautiful. Didn't give up when she didn't believe me.

I didn't know I loved her until I found myself in the middle of it.
Concern wasn't something I'd ever really thought about before.
Now all I could do was be concerned about her, and hope she cared.

It wasn't easy. There are tears inside her that nobody can stop.
But there are so many other things. I could show them to her.
That there's more to life than more. And there's more to life than less.

Talking to her, I felt strong in a different way. Without her, I faltered.
I felt alone again, with so many questions and no one to ask.
I found that with love, you need someone to talk to about it.

There were guys on the team, but their girlfriends didn't like Mary.
They always had someone else to set me up with, to bring me back.
The guys' allegiance was to the team, and the girls had to take it.

The guys wanted to hear about my sex life, not my love life.
John kept asking me for "the details," and at first I told him.
But when I saw he didn't care what they linked up to, I stopped.

The guys would make jokes, about her size, about our sex.
I never really laughed, but no one noticed. Until I started to hold back.
Until I started to tell them to go on without me.

Coach pulled me aside, asked me where my fire had gone.
He told me to bulk up, to add the shakes and supplements—
everything short of steroids. Just like John and Bo and Tray and Dex.

What's lonelier than being on a team where you no longer belong?
Even though I was catching passes, I was losing the bigger game.
John started making more jokes. And he was my best friend.

If it had happened to someone else, would I have done the same?
I found myself asking this question, and was saddened by the answer.
When John pretended to screw her, I knew I'd be gone by wrestling.

She said, *Don't make me your everything.* I knew she was right.
As she got better, as my feelings shifted from concern to care,
I could also feel the space between us shift, our levels of need.

I used to talk to Daniel, but he was gay now, different.
We had talked about things, but they weren't important things.
Important then, yes. But no longer as important now. Different.

Maybe this is what happens when life is no longer about bodies.
You find yourself in your own body, and no matter how strong it is,
it is separate. It contains its own space. It must find its own way.

And maybe it is only by finding yourself separate that you can feel
the true intensity of becoming close to another person.
I am trying to understand this, and I am trying to understand it with her.

The day I quit the team, the day I leave all that, I will cry in her arms.
I will be the same body I was before, the same body I will be after.
But at that moment I won't believe I have a body at all, just a proximity.

To get something, you must give something away.
To hold something, you must give something away.
To love something, you must give something away.

The Patron Saint of Stoners

I know all the novels of Jane Austen
The quadratic equation
Heisenberg's Principle of Uncertainty.
I know how to conjugate four languages
All the periods of Picasso
And the reasons Jane Grey was beheaded.
But I don't know where the hell
To find some pot.

It's not in the student handbook.
It won't be on any AP exam
Or as a word problem on the SATs—
Finding pot is to Clara as
Giving birth is to a man.

My mother wouldn't have had this problem
When she was my age, I'm sure she knew every source
Hanging out in the parking lot pick-ups
Blasting the radio to some tune that's now an oldie.
That's how I see it, she is so sure of herself
And she has no more understanding of me then
Than I do of her now.

I go to Jed because he's probably my only friend
With more than a passing knowledge of marijuana.

He's friends with so many people that it baffles me.
I guess I am his token Socially Inept But Intelligent friend
Or at least I would be if he wasn't friends with
All the other Socially Inept But Intelligent people in our class.

I know he won't laugh at me
Or ask too many questions.
I don't know which I am more afraid of.
The truth is laughable.
And the truth isn't funny at all.

One time my mother told me she had this friend named Leo
Who carried a hula hoop around with him at school.
He kept everything inside of it. Chapters from his textbooks,
Coins for a soda. Even a comb that he'd filed down to fit.
I think my mother was in love with Leo, at least a little.
He would let her twirl the hoop with her waist and
She would hear all of his possessions turning around her.
Then they'd go outside and get stoned, or at least
That's what my mother told me.

I tell Jed I've never understood the word "stoned."
I thought the whole purpose of smoking pot
Was to find a kind of lightness, to lift a burden.
This is my way of introducing the subject.
He says he never understood the term "pot" either
Since it's not like you're boiling the weed.
I hear "weed" and wish that finding pot
Was as easy as picking dandelions in the park.

I say, "If I wanted to find some, where would I?"
I don't add, "It's not for me," because I swore to myself
I wouldn't say that, couldn't say that, even to Jed.
Jed looks at me curiously, but is going to play along.
"You'd go to Toby," he says. "You know Toby."
And I tell him it depends on the definition, because
Of course I know who Toby is, but I haven't spoken to him
Since we had recess together—the kind with jungle gyms.
"Do you want me to ask him?" Jed offers. But I say
No, I have to take care of this myself.

I think my mother has this line she's made for herself.
She'll tell me she's done drugs, but she won't tell me
What it was like. She doesn't want to make them sound good
But the stories with drugs are always the exciting ones.
I think she was high when she met my father,
Which would explain a lot of what happened next.
Because even I know that a high isn't something you can keep
Day to day. They were at a concert and she fell in love
With his shirt. I've seen the shirt in the back of the closet
At his house. It's yellow and purple. It makes no sense.

Toby is not a bad guy. He's just not my kind of guy.
I think the only thing we have in common is that
We both hate gym. When people make the distinction
Between "smart" and "intelligent," he is an example of "smart"
And I am an example of "intelligent." He carries a knapsack
Covered with buttons for bands whose names seem to come
From the Dictionary of Contentious Words. He sleeps in class,

Wakes neighbors at night. The principal knows him by first name
But can never nail him for anything more than his attitude.

I walk over to him on the sidelines at gym, even as
I realize that not even Toby would have pot in his gym clothes.
"What's up?" he asks, like we talk all the time.
"Not much," I reply automatically. Then I teeter
And am about to walk away when he says,
"Did you want to ask me something?"
Not like he knows the answer. I'm speechless, so he says,
"You looked like you wanted to ask me something."
And I say, "I need to get some pot."
Just like that. I expect alarms to go off,
All the kids on the field to stop and gape.
I expect to have become a lesser person.
Or at least for Toby to be surprised.
But he just says, "Not here. How much?"

I have no idea. He prompts me,
"A nickel? A dime? A quarter?"
And I have no clue whether he's talking cost
Or some other measure. So I just say,
"A half-dollar," and he whistles like I'm
A real player. "Come over at four," he says.
And I nod, thinking as I walk back to pick up
My field hockey stick that this is the first time
That a boy's asked me over in a while.

My mother likes to say she was never a genius
Because she probably killed too many brain cells.
From the way she says it, I know she thinks
I am most probably a genius, and I have
Way too many brain cells left.
She is always telling me to have fun.
I want to ask her when she last had fun.
But that would be too mean.

There is nothing honorable about Honors Society.
We meet once a month and talk about what
We're going to put on our transcripts, always
Leaving off one or two things, so we'll be underestimated.
I'm sure nobody misses me when I don't show up.
They probably assume I am at home studying.
Or volunteering with the elderly. Or doing something prodigal
With a violin. I doubt they think I am heading to Toby's
To buy some pot with the money I was saving
For a prom dress that's seven months and one boyfriend away.

I look in Toby's garage to see if his parents are home,
Although maybe that doesn't matter. Maybe they know.
Their industrious son answers the door in his boxer shorts
And an unmarked T-shirt. He asks me in and offers me
Something to drink. I decline. I am so nervous
But I realize he's not the one making me nervous.
He is so casual. So sure of himself. I would buy
A nickel of that, a dime, a hundred-dollar bill.
He reaches into a drawer and pulls out a baggie of pot.

And I think it's remarkable that he trusts me
To keep quiet, to never give the principal his name.
He trusts me as easily as he trusts the bag to keep from breaking.

"It's really good stuff," he says. "I promise."
I wonder if it's enough and figure it probably is,
At least for now. I ask him how much, and he names a figure
That's more than nickels and dimes but still less than I'd imagined.
My hand is shaking as I reach into my purse
For my wallet the size of a filing cabinet.
"Coupons?" he asks. I nod. He smiles.
"I always forget to use them, too."
I pay him. He doesn't bother to count it.
My hand won't stop shaking and now my body
Is chiming in. "Are you okay?" he asks.
And I say what I swore I wouldn't say, which is,
"It's not really for me."

He doesn't question this. He just closes the drawer
And I know our conversation—our transaction—is
Complete. I thank him too much and he says,
"Anytime." And the way he says it is so gentle
So sweet that I'm afraid I am going to cry right there
In his foyer. His parents will come home and find
This sobbing girl with a baggie of pot in her purse.
I don't think he understands me at all, and
I admire him for not even trying. For letting me
Take a moment to make myself presentable
For an outside world that will remain outside
Even when I'm in it.

I wonder when my mother last had a joint. I wonder
If those nights when I'm hanging at friends', watching videos,
She's been toking up in the backyard, or even in her bedroom,
Turning on the fan so I won't notice the telltale smell.
Or maybe it was something she gave up,
Like my father, or their marriage, or my delinquency.
Should I have checked her eyes when she picked me up
From Quiz Bowl? Does it matter? That was a while ago.

I go straight home and don't have to look in the garage
To know she's around. There's a light on in her bedroom
That I see at all hours of the day. I throw down my bag,
Kick off my shoes, unravel myself from school.
I have drugs, I think, and smile at myself goofily in the mirror.
I can see the thrill of the sneaking, the stashing, the subterfuge.
But that's not my plan. I have five minutes to relish it,
Because I can hear my mother stirring upstairs,
Which means she hears me footstepping downstairs.
I pick up my bag, pick up my shoes, and head to her.
The door is open. There is nothing in the silence of the house
To disturb her.

And even though I am used to this
Even though I should be used to this
For a second I think this is not
My mother just lying here like a body
Barely a person, almost a ghost
Strength as thin as paper
Breathing harbored underneath
Labored, saddened, closed

Eyes that speak for all the senses.
This is not my mother
It is who my mother becomes
When the treatment doesn't work
When the future's eyes are closed.

But then she senses I'm in the room
And she opens her eyes and sits up against
The throne of pillows I've left her to.
"Clara," she says, her voice so many things wrong.
And I tell her I've brought her something
To ease the pain. I move closer
Pulling the baggie out. At first she doesn't understand.
Then there's recognition. Surprise. My name, this time,
Is a full exclamation. "Clara Barger! Is that?!"
She laughs and hugs me and opens the baggie,
Probing her fingers inside, then inhaling like an old pro.
"Good stuff," she says. And the delight in her eyes
Is my idea of heaven. I have done this one thing right.

She asks me if I have rolling papers, and then quickly tells me
Not to worry, she has some of her own. When she doesn't tell me
Where they are, which of her drawers, I know that I am not going
To be a part of this. This is something she is going to do alone.
She tells me I've done enough already, that she is happy.
Even without it lit, she bends her head and inhales.
Closes her eyes, but this time she is not a patient, my father's ex,
Or even my mother. She is ducking out to the parking lot.
She is holding the hand of a day she never felt she'd touch
Again.

We always hug before I leave the room.
This time it wraps me a little more.
The sun hasn't gone down yet
But she's saying goodnight, she's saying
She has some evening plans. I tell her
To have fun, to not do anything I wouldn't do.
Which is a lie, and we both know it.
That night as I type a paper about Emerson
And talk on the phone to a boy who's only good for
Calculus, my mother blasts the stereo so loud I think
The neighbors will complain, and the air lingers
With a spice and a flame this house hasn't known
For years, unless you count dreams.

In school the next day
I talk about the novels of Jane Austen
The quadratic equation
Heisenberg's Principle of Uncertainty.
I conjugate four languages
Discuss all the periods of Picasso
And the reasons Jane Grey was beheaded.
But like always all I'm really thinking about
Is a bedroom with a woman sick inside.
Today I picture her toking up,
Smiling over the pain.
Please put that on my transcript.

In gym, I don't see him, but when I'm walking home
Toby appears at my side. He says, "Hey,"

And takes something out of his backpack.
It's a Gap bag, but I can tell there's another bag
Inside. I didn't know I'd signed up for a daily
Delivery service. I am annoyed
At myself. "I don't have any money," I say,
"I can't." He smiles and says, "Take it."
We stop and he unzips my bag and puts the pot inside.
"I'll have to pay you tomorrow," I protest.
And he shakes his head.
"Just take it." "But I don't want it."
And then he says,
"It's not for you."
And I know
He knows exactly what's going on. My secret
Is so much less a secret than I ever thought.
He does the most unbelievable thing then
Right there in the middle of the road
He gives me the biggest hug and I just about fall
Apart. How can I
Thank
Protest
Comprehend
Him? He won't give me a chance
He nods once
Acknowledging me
Then walks away.

four

Charlotte

Elizabeth

Cara

Lia

Writing

I've always put thoughts in the margins. Some pages are all margins—just the words thrown down and recorded wherever they land. I have spent most of my time in high school doing this. Sometimes a word or two from the teacher will break through. But not often. Instead I just think through the pen. Whatever comes. I won't even try to explain it. There is no need to explain it. Some people like to doodle cartoon animals and other people write notes to other people. Fine for them. I've never been like that. It is always raining in my head. The closest thing I have to order is the way the lines are set on the pages. But even those I disregard. And then one day I jump right off. Instead of turning the page I just start writing on the desk. All that open surface. Right there. Nobody notices. Nobody cares. The words just start to fall there. And I feel some satisfaction from that. I've never written just for myself. And I've never written for anyone else. I write for the release of it. For finding out what will be there when I am done. The desk is the dull yellow that can only be found in school furniture. My ink is the blue that can be found anywhere. I don't even give thought to what I am writing. THERE IS NO MEASURE TO VOLATILITY. I write it again and again. No idea where it's coming from. The appeal is that one word. VOLATILITY. Next period that is all I write. VOLATILITY. Carved so hard I almost break my pen. Stains the side of my hand. Nobody notices. But I know the people who come in the following periods will have to notice. Will have to think about it. Even if they are just going to dismiss it. The next day works the same way. I get a sentence. COMMISERATE WITH THE COMMON. And then I pare it down to a word. COMMISERATE. This time someone notices. This guy named Daniel leans over and asks What's That? I tell him I have no idea. He nods as if that makes sense. The girl in English isn't as cool. She says You Know You Really Shouldn't Be Doing That. So I write YOU ARE UNABLE TO COMMISERATE. She looks like she wants to tattle. But she doesn't want to be that uncool. Something about the YOU ARE grabs me. The next day I write YOU ARE HAPPY EVEN IF YOU ARE AFRAID TO ADMIT IT. And it makes sense. Because how many times have I heard everyone complaining and complaining and complaining? As if sitting back and acknowledging that things aren't all that bad is somehow wrong. Then I write YOU ARE FOOLISH IN YOUR UNHAPPINESS. Nobody wipes off the previous days' messages. They accumulate like skid marks. Sometimes they intersect like answers in a crossword puzzle. It gets crowded. I start writing on walls. I KNOW THIS IS NOT A SOCIALLY ACCEPTABLE THING TO DO. I start in the bathrooms because it is more hidden there. Sneaking into the stall. Avoiding the blow job notices and the anonymous insults. YOU ARE NOT WHO YOU BELIEVE YOU ARE. That one gets to me. I sit there on the toilet and stare at it long enough to miss the late bell. I try to convince myself that I don't believe in who I am. Even though I know that itself is a belief. I take the phrase outside. Hit the hallways when everyone else is in class. Write small. People start to notice. There is a mystery to it. I think people will know right away that it is me. The desks haven't been cleaned off. The evidence is right there. But I think at first people like that it's a

mystery. YOU WEAR TOO MANY MASKS. It would be easy
to simply baffle them with jibberish—The Walrus Walks At
Midnight. But that's not what the margins have been about.
I want to make sense. One day all I can write is the word PLEASE.
Over and over again. Above mirrors. Beside fire extinguishers.
PLEASE. I have to be careful now. Teachers are starting to frown
on it. The janitors clean off the desks. They try to erase the walls.
YOU SHOULD NOT HIDE, I write. Those are the words that
come. Are they addressing me or everyone else? I just put them up
and walk away. People start to become uneasy. I don't know how
to describe it. I walk in between classes and see people gathered
and staring. GIVE HER A CHANCE. And the bizarre thing is that
I can see some people are finding meaning in it. Like I'm posting
bulletins from the truth. YOU SHOULD NOT WALK AWAY
QUITE YET. Like the trick of flipping the coin. When what you're
really doing is seeing if you agree or disagree with the outcome.
Or the fortune teller's wisdom. Knowing the vague is the universal.
Knowing that we all have these things in common. The word
PLEASE means something to us all. We are all so damn insecure.
With unease comes hostility. People start to cross me out. The
Principal makes an announcement. Daniel asks It's You, Isn't It?
But I know he won't tell. He is intrigued. PROTECT ME FROM
WHAT I WANT. It's that girl. I know it is. Amber something. The
next day's announcement is for me and me alone. So I go down to
the office. But not before stopping around the corner. Pen ready.
The first word: LIVE. The second word: UP. The third: TO.
The fourth: YOURSELF. The Principal doesn't care what I've been
writing. He says it's where I've been writing it. I am to clean every
last word. Erase every last thought. Strange, I don't mind. I know

I've only been borrowing the walls. I know the thoughts have grown old. So I sponge. And I whitewash. The next day I am back with my notebook. COWARDICE, I write. This time I know it's directed at me. Perhaps directed *by* me as well. I cannot push the words back in the margins. So I start to write on my jeans. DESPAIR IS NOT THE ANSWER. People look at me strangely. A few ask me what it's about. And I tell them I don't know. Some tell me to keep going. Others tell me to stop. Not nicely. I find the words will not come out in the wash. Across the inside of my arm I write YOU ARE IMPLICATED. People stop me in the hall. They stare. One girl actually grabs my wrist. Reads my arm. Asks me Why Are You Doing This? Who Do You Think You Are? I can feel her hinges loosening. I don't know what it means. We are so used to releasing words. We don't know what to do with them if they stay. Not on the walls. I'm not talking about the walls. I'm talking about what happens when they stay with us. No matter how many times we let them go, they come back. The words that matter always stay.

Your Sister

1.

My first days of high school, I wanted to change
my last name, I wanted my own identity.
Not because everybody hated you, but because
they loved you so much, and I was not you.

You had just left and I had just arrived,
and I could no more take your place
than a noontime shadow can take the shape
of the body that leaves it behind.

Mr. Delaney was new, so I could not remind him
of you. But the rest of the teachers
were soon disappointed that I had not studied
you better, had not learned the same things.

I could not live up, so I lived down
the boys who passed their crushes on to me,
the girls who wanted me to join things
so they could be in charge of me as you were of them.

I wanted you more than ever
to have never existed.
I was the keeper of a flame
that had never been lit.

2.

It's not that you hadn't taught me things
or that I hadn't listened. When I got my schedule in May,
you talked me through from teacher to teacher,
telling me your version of the truth.

You could flirt your way to extensions
with Mr. Peterson, while Mrs. Platt would rather
stick a fork in your ear than answer a question twice.
Mr. Rose gave the same tests every year.

Mrs. Green had been sweet to you, and
(you promised) would be sweet to me, too.
What I should've known was this said more about you
than it did about her, and nothing really about me.

This was the one time we talked about high school
since you were already planning for college.
My change was a matter of streets while yours
was a matter of latitudes.

I could not compete, so didn't.
I dove into your preparations,
went shopping for a wastebasket and a microwave,
which would be going with you instead of me.

This was how we'd always played.
You were Cinderella, I was a mouse.

You were Alice, I was the Hatter.
You were the sun, and I wasn't even the moon.

I loved being the supporting character,
because I felt it was my way of supporting you.
I asked for nothing in return
and wanted so much.

3.

I pierced my ear four times
and ditched my old friends,
the girls who idolized you
to the point of missing me.

When Andy Reilly told me
I looked as good as you
he meant it as a compliment
and I told him to get lost.

He told *me* to get lost
then called me that night
to say it again.
We laughed, and I was free.

You told me about boys but always waited
to tell me about the ones who you liked.
You treated me like a direct line to Mom

when all I wanted was to keep your secrets.

When I was twelve, I was too old for a baby-sitter
and you were too old to be a baby-sitter.
But Mom and Dad shackled us with allowances,
so I became your Saturday night burden, and you mine.

Then Mike Reilly came over with flowers
and I knew something was going to happen.
I watched the TV and tried to listen to you
murmuring in the other room.

You left me with two slices of pizza and a soda.
You left me with a look and the door closed.
I was smart enough to know, but not enough to be angry.
You left me and wouldn't even say where you were going.

4.

Even after you were away, I heard things.
Those barbed admirations from girls
you probably didn't know all that well
but who felt they'd figured you inside out.

You call from college and talk to me first
if I happen to be the one who answers the phone.
You ask how it is, and you're asking about your absence.
You say to fill you in, but you're not empty.

I try to picture you in the halls you've left to me—
it looks like a parade, everyone celebrating you.
I keep my head down, try to play
the girl who doesn't say hello.

Andy says he remembers you
coming over, charming his parents.
He remembers when you ended it, how Mike tore
at his shelves and broke his books.

And I tell him the truth—that you
cried for days and screamed at me
when my music got too loud, as if
I was flooding you with love songs.

I wonder what you would think of me
and Andy. I imagine you would approve
and I don't want to care about that.
I want to keep my own secret now.

5.

I go into your room at night
and search the walls for clues.
You are my glimpse of the future
and I don't really know you at all.

6.

The worst is Cara Segal, fulfilling
her reputation as the worst.
You'd think a senior would have better things to do
than to search me out for taunts.

At first it's just comments, calling me
your runt, your clone, a slut like my sister.
She wears her jealousy in a rage,
looking at me and seeing you.

I want you there to defend me.
I want you there to show there are two of us.
I want you there because I don't know what to do
and I am sure you'd know exactly.

But you are thousands of people away.
So when Cara tells Andy and everyone else
that I am history repeating, that I will
kill his heart recklessly, I must take her on myself.

He doesn't believe her, but I don't like her
saying it. So I find her in the cafeteria
and belt her with an orange plastic tray.
It's not what you would do, but it works.

Being suspended is an unexpected reward.
I am suddenly considered

another kind of person.
And I *am* that kind of person, if provoked.

When I get out of the principal's office
Andy is by my locker with flowers
he skipped seventh period to buy.
He carries them on an orange plastic tray.

7.

I do not want to be your history repeating
but you are my history nonetheless.
I do not want you to be my guide
but I want to see which way you went.

I come home and Mom is on the phone,
relaying the news to you with concern.
You ask to speak to me, and I expect
another sermon of disapproval.

But instead you say *way to go*
and tell me you should have smacked Cara
when you'd had the chance.
You are proud of me.

I don't want you to be my definition,
and still I want you to mean something to me.
I have lost having you here, and here
you are, saying I am going to be a star.

8.

The year you left, I was always missing you.
Your life was moving so fast
away from me, and I could only
grab hold so much, so tight.

But there were moments when you were still
with me, and it is these moments I gather
when I try to summon you, conjure you.
I tell Andy the stories, like the night of your prom.

I remember how you came into my room after midnight.
You were still Cinderella, ball-adorned
in the quarterlight of the hour.
You told me to follow you outside.

So we crept down the sleeping stairs
careful not to wake anything but the folds of your dress,
which fell effortlessly, carelessly to the ground,
clearing the path for my bare footsteps.

I would have followed you anywhere
and you took me to our backyard,
to where the swing set used to preside,
the place you taught me to move my legs to go higher.

I whispered when I asked you how the dance was
and you whispered back a word so soft
I felt you were talking in a dream language

I was too young and too nervous to know.

Before I could ask you more, you bent your knees,
sat down, lay back on the grass in your pearl-colored dress,
telling me to slip beside you, to be quiet and stare
at something far enough away to make my thoughts rise.

I still do not know why you wanted me there,
what made you think of me at that moment.
But as I felt the damp ground against my nightgown
you reached over and let your hand rest on mine.

Above there were stars and planets,
distant bodies so intriguing and elusive,
formed like a pattern across night's ceiling,
a map to all that I could not reach.

A car might have passed, crickets may have sung . . .
all I can remember is the silence.
When I turned to look at you, I was afraid to move again—
the moment was just too beautiful to be lost.

Comeuppance

She broke my nose. The doctors said
she didn't, that the bruise would go away.
But I could tell. It was different than it was
before. If I held a photo next to the mirror
I didn't match. Not perfectly.

It hurt. The moment of impact, sure.
That tray coming out of nowhere,
smashing me in the face. But that didn't hurt
as much as the moment after. Looking around
and seeing how pleased everyone was.
How much they enjoyed it, as I bled.

Nobody deserves that. Think I'm a total
bitch, whatever. I don't care. I tell it
like it is, and some people can't deal
with that. That's no reason to make me bleed,
and enjoy it. I could see the satisfaction
on her face, and on everyone else's.

It hadn't been like that before. When Jill stole
Roger from right under my nose, at my
birthday party—well, I had everybody's
sympathy then. Or when Mr. Cooper tried
to attack me in front of the whole class

for refusing to read out loud the note
he'd caught me writing to Amber—I was
cheered for finally putting him in his place.

So this came out of nowhere.

Of course, my friends offered their
condolences. Worked themselves into
a lather of retribution, then moved on
to other things, like facials.
(Ooh, sorry, Cara, we know you
won't be able to get one with us,
not with that bandage and all.)

I believe in having a code of ethics,
and mine was basically: If you
jerk me around, then I will jerk you
right back, harder. But I found that
because that girl had attacked me
so openly, my credibility was gone.
Nobody would believe a word I said
about her, not even an innuendo.

Every day, I called the doctor and begged
for him to take the tape off my face.
Do you want it misaligned? he asked,
and I knew instantly that he'd been
unpopular in high school, which was why
he'd branded me with this scarlet *Loser*

to walk the halls with. It wasn't even
the kind of bruise guys find brave.

I complained to Amber, told her I hadn't
deserved this. After all, I'd only been trying
to warn that boy Andy. I remembered
what her sister had done to his brother.
I remember Mike being so sad that he couldn't
understand when I tried to comfort him.
I wasn't saying anything that wasn't a *fact*.
I had his best interests at heart.

Amber just nodded, told me I was right.
I don't even think she was listening.
And while I know I should have been
grateful for her unquestioning loyalty—
she was simply assuming I was right, after all—
it still got to me. I reminded her that I was
the one who had warned her about Jakob.
Sure enough, he cheated on Brenda
two weeks later. *That could have been you,*
I reminded her. She sighed, said whatever.

I tried to be a vigiliant person. Keeping watch,
confronting people with the truth, even if
it hurt them. In the long run, it was always better
to know. That's what I believed. The poison
cure. Then one day, right after my bandage
had come off, I got to English class and found

something written on my desk: YOU ARE
UNABLE TO COMMISERATE. Other words
had been written there, too. But I hadn't noticed
them until this sentence appeared.

I looked around. Who had done this
to me? Why would they say that?
I wanted to stand up right there and say
I am a very commiserating person,
thank you very much. But luckily
I stopped myself. I realized that the words
weren't meant for me. Just something
written on a desk, some jerk venting.

That should have been that. But the words
stayed with me. When I sat down the next day
there was something else: YOU ARE HAPPY
EVEN IF YOU ARE AFRAID TO ADMIT IT.
And the opposite happened. I realized that
the words *weren't* meant for me, and that struck me
just as hard. I took the bottled water out of my bag
and tried to wipe the words away. It was no use.
No matter how hard I tried, they wouldn't leave
me alone. I saw people looking, wondering why
I was attacking my desk with a wet tissue. I stopped.

I knew Amber had English the period before me,
so I asked her if she'd seen anything. She said
yes, this obnoxious goth girl liked to write things

all over her desk. *Does she know me?* I asked,
and Amber looked at me like I was out of my mind.
I got to English early the next day, and saw
who she meant. This depressing girl, so far beyond
a makeover. I stood there by the door as she left,
waiting for some kind of recognition. When she
passed by, I was relieved, and a little disappointed.

But there it was on the desk again—YOU ARE
FOOLISH IN YOUR UNHAPPINESS. This time
I just snapped. *Why is she doing this?* As I felt
my unhappiness collecting in my throat. *Why
am I doing this?* It still hurt to breathe sometimes,
with the broken nose and all. Now it was a different
kind of hurt. I felt foolish, yes. Foolish because
I felt alone in this. How many times had I told
someone *The truth hurts.* Without ever really
knowing what it felt like, until that stupid desk.

I switched seats. I tried to block it out. I looked
at the boy who took my place, and he didn't seem
fazed. Then the words started to appear other places.
Sitting in a stall, doing my business, when suddenly
I look up and see YOU ARE NOT WHO YOU BELIEVE
YOU ARE. The same handwriting. Waiting for me.
I thought of that question—*Who do you think you are?*—
and realized that it's not one you ever get a chance
to answer. I tried to answer it, right there in the stall.
I am a good friend. I am a truth seeker. I am a

bitch. A gossip. Someone who gets hit with a tray
in the middle of the cafeteria and gets no sympathy.
And I thought *If I'm not any of these things, what am I?*

I tried to talk to Amber about it, but she said flat out
that I shouldn't let any loser's graffiti get into my head.
They're all out to get us, she said. And when I asked why,
she just sighed and said, *Because we're better, I guess.*
We have what they want. Two weeks ago, the same words
would have come from my mouth. Now they seemed empty.
I didn't feel any better. YOU WEAR TOO MANY MASKS
was written over my locker the following day. This time,
I had an answer. I thought, *No, I only wear one.*
People were starting to talk about the writing. Everyone
seemed to think it was about them. A personal attack.
The old me had to admire the way this girl had managed
to get under everyone's skin all at once.

Some days it was just one word. PLEASE or ANYTHING.
One day it was PROTECT ME FROM WHAT I WANT.
What I wanted was everything to go back to when my
nose was straight and my behavior unquestioned (at least
by me). I saw Andy and that girl who hit me walking the halls
together, happy. I saw her balance his books on her head
while he looked for something in his locker. I could have
knocked them off as I passed. One simple mean reach.
But instead I stayed in the background, alone.

I went the long way through school, trying to collect
all the phrases. I wondered if the goth girl kept a list.
YOU SHOULD NOT WALK AWAY QUITE YET.
When I found that one, in a corner outside the auditorium,
I sat down and stared. Because what I wanted
to walk away from was myself. In fact, I felt I'd already
started. I took a bottle of nail polish out of my purse
and traced the letters. This sophomore passed by and gave me
a strange look. I told him to get lost. Then I dipped
the brush in again, turned a W red. The smell of the
nail polish made me think of Amber and the rest of
my friends. I missed them, but in theory. It wasn't
them I missed, but friendship. QUITE YET.

I learned the goth girl's name when the principal called
her down to the office. Charlotte Marshall. The words
stopped coming. I didn't know what to do. I sat
at the same lunch table, I went to the same classes.
I stopped talking and nobody noticed, not unless
there was something spiteful to be said. Amber asked me
if I had gone on medication. Liza offered me some of
her own. My mother took me shopping. I didn't
know what to do with the four shirts I bought.
Well, I knew to wear them. But it all seemed part
of the mask. Was there anything underneath?

A few days later, I saw Charlotte walking down
the hallway. I saw writing on her arm, and before
I knew what I was doing, I reached out

for her wrist. YOU ARE IMPLICATED, it said.
And suddenly I was asking her *What do you mean?*
She looked at me, not knowing. *Why are you*
doing this? She shrugged and I let go of her wrist.
I was shocked: she didn't have any more answers
than I did. She just knew how to raise the questions.

That night, I locked myself in the bathroom.
I let the water run, stood in front of the mirror.
Then I took out the box of Crayola markers
I'd had in my desk since I was a little kid.
Most of them had dried out, but the green still wrote.
I started on the inside of my arms. YOU ARE
IMPLICATED. YOU ARE FOOLISH
IN YOUR UNHAPPINESS. YOU ARE NOT
WHO YOU BELIEVE YOU ARE. YOU WEAR
TOO MANY MASKS. I tried her handwriting,
but ended up with my own. PROTECT ME
and I ran out of room. I turned over my arm
FROM WHAT I WANT.

My legs were next. In big letters. YOU ARE
UNABLE TO COMMISERATE. YOU ARE
UNABLE TO WALK AWAY. YOU HAVE
NO ONE. YOU ARE NO ONE. I had forgotten
what else she'd written. I was on my own now.
YOU ARE FULL OF SPITE. YOUR FRIENDS
ARE NOT REAL. YOU HAVE PUT YOURSELF
IN THIS CORNER. THERE IS NO ESCAPE.

The steam rising now. I took off my shirt
and skirt, stood there in my underwear.
BITCH. LIAR. LOSER. UGLY. SAD.
I wish I could say it felt good, but it felt
horrible. STOP CRYING. STOP IT NOW.
YOU WILL GO TO COLLEGE AND
EVERYBODY WILL HATE YOU.
THIS IS THE TRUTH. DEAL WITH IT.

All of these things had been inside me.
Now they were spelled out, upside down
so I could read them. Backwards in the mirror.
I was ready to put down the pen, give up.
But there was something else inside me, too.
YOU ARE NOT BEING FAIR, it wrote.
YOU CAN BE LOYAL. YOU CAN BE
STRONG. YOU ARE SMART. YOU KNOW
HOW THINGS WORK. The words were
beginning to overlap. The marker was fading
with every new letter. YOU KNOW WHAT
YOU HAVE TO DO on the bottom of my foot.
Then I did something one of the metalheads
at school always does. HATE on the knuckles
of one hand. LOVE across the other.

I laughed when I saw myself in the mirror.
I stared long and hard, so I would remember.
Then I slipped into the tub. The water turned
green instantly. I drained it out, let new water

in. It was so hot I could barely tell the difference
between my sweat and the steam. But I got
used to it. I looked down at myself and most of
the words were still there. I closed my eyes and
I remembered what it was like when I was younger.
The night before the first day of school, I would
stand under the shower and make all kinds of
resolutions. *I will make new friends. I will
be more popular. I will get good grades.*
And I swear I can remember, *I will be
a better person.* At some point I stopped doing this.
Maybe I forgot. Or maybe I knew the resolutions
never carried over when I got to school.

I WILL BE A BETTER PERSON. I know
it's hard to believe. From me. From the bitch
who got pummeled with an orange tray.
But I knew—I hadn't become the worst kind
of person yet. I had to believe that. I took
down the washcloth and started scouring my skin.
Floods of soap. My skin raw under the rub.
The words vanishing, the letters erased.
Only a green-tinted reminder. A ring around
the tub once it emptied. A spot or two on my body
that I'd missed. On purpose, for now.

I did not apologize to Elizabeth, but I stopped
saying she owed me an apology. I did not ditch my friends.
I simply tried to shift the tone a little. It was hard

sometimes, not to attack. But I felt some strength
in the holding back. YOU WILL BE A BETTER
PERSON. I wrote it wherever I could. *What's
gotten into you?* Amber asked, looking at me
seriously for the first time in ages. And I said,
It's actually something that's gotten out of me.
She didn't understand, and I honestly didn't
expect her to. I have no more idea now of
who I am than I did before. But at least I know
that. And I'm starting to figure out who I want
to be. Whether it was the tray, Charlotte's words,
or something else that caused it to happen, all I can
say is this: Being a bitch is easy. It's finding
the alternative that's hard.

the grocer's daughter

the first delivery comes at six in
  the morning.
usually I sleep through its arrival,
leaning into the noise like a pillow,
thinking of it as a sound that's
  passing by.
but recently I have been rushing
to the window, lifting
the shade slightly to see him
get out of the truck, say hello
to my father, and lift the boxes
  into the store.

one day I woke up early
  and he was there.
one day I woke up early
  and kept waking early.

if I am very quiet I can hear him
  speaking Korean to my father.
it is not a language I learned.
instead it was grown
  inside me.
they talk about cantaloupes and
  tissue paper,

other grocers and their misfortunes.
sometimes he asks after my mother
    but never about me.
my father would not tell him
    about me, unless there was a reason
    to boast.

from my window, he is the most
    handsome boy.
he cannot be much older than me.
because of my parents, I cannot
    imagine
his parents would let him get out
    of school.
but I have never seen a book
near him or heard him talk about
    classes.
he must be older than me, but not
    by much.
this handsome boy is the one
    I pictured
when I was a girl and imagined
walking down a red-carpet aisle,
    delicate
blossoms in my hair, white as
    hope.

I come home from school
and I think of him

as I move the old milk cartons
    to the front
as I take the cigarette boxes from
    their cartons
as I sweep the floor
I do not ask his name.

as my father checks my homework
as my mother weighs the clove
    of garlic
as we pull the metal over our
    windows
as we tie the day's newspapers and
    throw them away
I ask for nothing
but these thoughts.

Clara catches me in my notebook.
I am tracing what I see when
    I close my eyes.
"who is that?" she asks, and then
she turns him so he is looking
    at her
and says, "that's really amazing."
even after I close him in my book
she asks me to tell her
through lunch and after school
so by the time we get to the store
I have told her what little

I know
and she is happy for me.
she gives me that look of advice
and says, "you should talk
    to him."

but he is gone by sunrise.
the morning after that
I get dressed early and move
    closer.
I am in the back room
on the other side of the door
breathing so loud I am sure he will
    hear
breathing the beat of my heart
as my father carries boxes
and makes morning jokes.
I see the boy in the space
    between the hinges
and that is enough like touching
for me to be happy.

Clara is always telling me
    about boys
the ones who are worthy
    of liking
and the rest who will disappoint
    you to tears.
I have felt things for other boys,

felt without falling.
friendship with Jed, because
   he was nice to me
flirtation with Michael, because
   he was Korean and safe
fluster for Simon, because
   he was not Korean and dangerous.
but none of those other boys were
   like this one.
nothing has ever felt this pure.

"you were up early," I tell my
   father,
tempting fate, tempting knowledge.
and he says, "you should get
some sleep, you need your
   sleep."
no mention of his early
companion, the boy who is not
his son, but could be his son
   in the future.

I am memorizing his shirts.
I am seeing the way he bends
   as he lifts.
on mornings when there is frost
I wipe a trail for him across the
   glass.
I see everything from above.

one day I will wake up and
he won't be there. he will
disappear as he appeared
and I will cry like a death
   foretold.
part of what I feel for him is
   missing him.
part of what I know is that
distance is as hard as it is
   easy.

I should talk to him.
I know I should talk to him
but I do not talk to him.
I watch him from afar
   and love him.

five

Zack

Karen

Lily

Jed

Experimentation

Last Thursday, I got carded at a sex shop.
The guy behind the counter explained to me
that I didn't have to be 18 to buy flavored condoms,
but I *did* need to be 18 to be in the store.
Luckily, I had my fake ID.

I'd never been inside that particular shop before.
It was called Lovely Pleasures, which sounded to me
like something you'd find on a Chinese menu.
At least it was better than the places called
ADULT VIDEO, which shows no imagination
whatsoever and makes you feel like you're
a dirty old man just for looking at the sign.

I like sex. I really do. And my girlfriend
likes sex. Which is convenient, I have to say.
We're always careful, we're always protected,
and basically we can't keep our bodies
off each other. We thrive on that intensity.

I was at the sex shop with Megan,
who is not my girlfriend but is
Diana's girlfriend now, I guess.
We didn't think Diana would ever
get over Elizabeth enough to be with Megan.

And maybe she hasn't. But they're giving
it a try anyway. Giving sex a try, that is.

I have known Meg since we were on tricycles,
and the most flavored things we knew were
Popsicles. I think it's safe to say that when
our mothers sat by the side of the pool and pictured our
futures, an aisle of prophylactics wasn't on their mind.

But we've grown up with each other, and we're
growing up with each other, too. So when she said
she needed help, I took out my keys and drove us to
Lovely Pleasures. It was either that or the drugstore,
and we know half the people who work at the drugstore.

Anne and I are always looking for new ways to go.
It's amazing the things that bodies can do.
The complicated ways that we fit.
I have seen her body naked dozens of times
and each time it is still an exploration.
Even when the bodies know, there is more to know.

The first time we had sex was in her bedroom
and she seemed more worried about me
messing up her great-grandmother's quilt
than anything else. All through the foreplay
she kept looking at it, shifting it so it wouldn't
feel our sweat. Until finally I pulled away
and folded it nicely, put it on a chair away from us.

It was not the first time for either of us,
but it was our first time with each other,
and that made it beautiful. Bright afternoon,
light of day through the shades,
basking in the sun-shadow of our affections.

That day, that moment, opened a curiosity of bodies,
shaped us as irrevocably as our first kiss, our first
realizations. You go into that moment never really knowing
if the closeness will wear well, if it is something that should
happen. I know she wasn't sure of me, and I wasn't sure
of me, either. But we discovered something in the unspoken,
found care in our caring whispers, instinctive.

I have not told Meg any of this, but she knew
right away when things had changed.
And it made her even sadder to know
I had found it while she was still waiting
for Diana to figure things out.

I don't know how the tide of Elizabeth
ebbed enough to show Meg standing on the shore.
But one day when Meg couldn't take it anymore,
she just put down Diana's guitar and walked away.
Diana asked me what was going on, and I didn't
have to say a word. She already knew, had maybe
known all along. Now it showed.

There was an e-mail that led to a phone call,
then a phone call that led to an encounter,
and an encounter that led to a tentative kiss.
I thought Meg would be happy, but instead
she was happy and very, very scared.

If you're not able to laugh inside a sex shop,
then you probably shouldn't be there.
I mean, they don't call it *fooling around* for nothing.
I was a little nervous that Meg would go skittish on me,
but instead we found ourselves laughing at the first
appliance we saw. Meg gravitated towards the costumes,
openly wondering about the nursewear.

Anne and I don't play roles when we're having sex.
She's the one I want to be with, not some fantasy.
When I close my eyes, I see her, and when I open them,
she is there. Nothing about us is anonymous.
This is the giving, the taking, the giving.

The first time I had sex was an opportunity I took.
And afterwards it didn't feel entirely right, like a trophy
I'd won because nobody else showed up. Some guys
can get off on this, and there were a lot of times before Anne
that I really wished I could. But for me, there has to be love.
Or at least the possibility of love. I wouldn't say Anne and I
love each other yet. But there are moments when we really do.

Meg has no doubts about her love. Only Diana's.
When love comes before sex, there's always the fear
that the sex will somehow undo the love.
With Anne and me, there could be the fear that the sex
is creating the love. I don't think that's the case.

Meg and I talked a little about this as we came to
a huge display of edible underwear.
Edible underwear is not something I can imagine
as tasting very good. Meg suggested we save
some money and make our skivvies out of
fruit leather instead. Gumdrop buttons, chocolate trim,
like a Hansel & Gretel house, only sexier.

As Meg checked out the body oils and incense,
I headed over to the condom area. The first time
I bought condoms was about a year before I used one.
Like thinking that shopping for summer clothes
will suddenly make the weather go warm.

I was so confused by all the sizes and styles—
I'd figured that a condom was a condom, and that was that.
(This wasn't exactly a father-son chat I'd had with my dad.)
How was I supposed to know my size?—it wasn't like getting
a new shoe, being measured by a salesman for the right fit.
I ended up getting the Greatest Hits Condom, extra-everything,
and kept it hidden inside an old Cracker Jack box.

In the sex shop, the sizes and styles were berserk-o,
but I was here for some experimentation, so that was okay.
Anne and I have reached the point in our relationship
where we're fueling it with little surprises—quick kisses,
notes hidden in pockets, glow-in-the-dark rubbers.

Meg and Diana haven't gotten to the little surprises yet.
I think they're still recovering from the big one.
We met up by the register, and she was holding candles
in different nail-polish colors, each promising its own
transcendent emotion—*luminescence* and *bliss* and
(my favorite) *astonishment*. I asked her if she was sure
she didn't want one of the "sculpted" candles and she laughed.

Then it was my turn and I got carded.
No big deal. Then we got back to the car
and everything that had been holding Meg up
fell right down. *I'm not ready for this,* she said.
And when I said that was okay, she added, *Any of it.*

Getting what you want is just as difficult
as not getting what you want. Because then
you have to figure out what to do with it
instead of figuring out what to do without it.
I did not feel the full depth of my wanting for Anne
until we were physically together, until it
was something so immediate it was beyond question.

There is wanting *it* so much, and there is wanting
her so much. Neither Meg or I want *it* as much
as we want *her.* In the car, bag of candles still on her lap,
Meg told me how afraid she was of things going wrong,
because this time it would be her fault, because of her wanting.

She said that maybe they should've stayed friends,
stayed safe behind the border of acting on desire.
So I asked, *Does kissing her make you want more?*
And she said, *Yes.* I asked *When you're sleeping
alone, do you wish she was there to touch?*
And she said, *Yes.* And I said, *There you go,* as if
those feelings were already taking her to the destination.

She didn't nod, didn't shake her head. Just looked out
the windshield. And I realized she hadn't needed me
to take her to a sex shop. This wasn't about sex,
but its complications. Our lives were taking
our friendship into a new territory.

So I told her that even though Anne and I really liked sex,
that even though we were learning each other's bodies
like they were our own, there was always a moment—
sometimes many—when I was scared that the desire
would reach its limit, that I would do or say the wrong thing,
that I was making myself vulnerably naked,
that my thoughts and hers would end up being opposites.

Then the fear would step back and I would feel
the hundreds of places where our skin was touching
and I would know that this was the sensation,
the metaphor for all the thoughts underneath.
I told Meg to remember this.
And I found myself telling her that the amazing thing
about seeing a woman naked is how open her body is,
how you can see right inside her. And it's astonishing
and complicated and intimidating and incredible.
All those layers to feel, to read. You look there
and you feel like you're knowing something,
even if you're not really sure what it is.

I don't know if this made her feel better
or just made her feel weird. We sat for a second
in silence, feeling Anne and Diana in the backseat
of our minds. Then she said *Jesus!* and started to
hug me. And I hugged her back.

What must we have looked like to someone
driving into the Lovely Pleasures parking lot?
Some guy and girl making out. When really we
were just a guy and a girl trying to make it through
our experimentations, trying to find the right balance
between love, sex, and the rest of it. Preparing for
our naked lives.

Unlonely

How to Be Alone

Remember that at any given moment
There are a thousand things
You can love

Plural

I had boyfriends non-stop
Since Greg Foster in fourth grade
I could only see myself through their eyes

The Last Breakup

Erased by the sex
Playing the role, badly
I was tired

What I Love (Three Examples)

Being myself
Being by myself
Flirting without consequences

What I Learned

The well-documented difference
Between alone and lonely
The comfort of knowing

R-E-S-P-E-C-T

What I need, baby, I got it
I used to define myself by the enthusiasm of kisses
Their enthusiasm, not mine

Singular

I only had one priority, then
Now I don't count them
I call my friends instead, talk about stupid fun things

A Cue from Nature

Run outside during a thunderstorm
That downpour, that conquered hesitation, that exhilaration
That's what unlonely is like

The Discovery

This is what my voice sounds like
I don't need to be talking to someone else
To hear it

escapade

At ten in the morning on a Saturday
    Jed shows up at my bedroom door and says

        Let's go on an escapade.

My parents have let him in
    so he can take me
        wherever we want to go.

I get dressed and put on my shoes.

        I'm no dummy.

Where shall we gallivant? he asks.

    These words are our thing.

Enrapture me with some possibilities, I reply.

He smiles.

    We can promenade, dither, roustabout, effervesce,
        or spiral.

I tell him I'll do anything but spiral.

   spiraling is what I do without Jed.

      although the spiraling I do isn't really a spiral.

         it only goes in

               one

                   d

                  ir

                    ec

                      tio

                        n

Jed says we'll promenade, and I make sure I have the right shoes for it.

      pink sneakers, yellow laces.

    He whistles his appreciation.

I have no idea how he knows when I need him. We can go weeks without speaking, and then, when my blue moods threaten to turn black, he will show up and tell me my moods are

     azure

     indigo

     cerulean

     cobalt

     periwinkle

      and suddenly the blue will not seem so dark, more
      like the color of a noon-bright sky.

                He brings the sun.

We drive past the mall, past the video store, past the TGI Friday's
past the movie theater, past the park, past the diner.

(We do not hang out in those places.
They are for other people.)

All of Jed's mixes have themes
and the one that's playing begins

red hot chili peppers—under the bridge
simon & garfunkel—bridge over troubled water
everything but the girl—another bridge
ani difranco—buildings and bridges

so I have a good idea where we're going. Jed will easily drive
an extra fifty miles to fit a theme.

I could not think of a more rhapsodic way to span a day with you, I say.

He smiles and tells me, **You're such a good egg.**

Jed will show up at my house with a thousand toothpicks,
and together we'll make a house for a salt-shaker family.

I will call him up and tell him I'm about to dye my hair purple
and he'll drive over with a box of purple crayons.

Our friendship is made of bendy straws, long midnight letters,
  my so-called life marathons, sleepless sleepovers,
  diner milk shakes, apron strings, a belief in beauty,
  sucking helium, and the most trust I've ever felt for
  anyone, including myself.

We roll down the windows and sing at the top of our lungs. Neither of
us can carry a tune, so we let the tune carry us instead.

Has your life been swell of late? he yells over the song, over me singing.

  Copacetic, with some rays of gloomy, I reply.

 Bugger the gloom! he declares. **What this-'n'-that is under disputation?**

   Just the usual bouts, I tell him.

    What about the bouts? he asks. **Are they
    caused by louts?**

   Just my own devout shouts.

   Well, we must shout them out!

    and with that we yell at the top of
    our lungs. It is unacceptable
    to sit in your room alone and
    scream at your life, but it is
    perfectly acceptable (albeit not

exactly normal) to do it with
a good friend on the highway,
hearing your voice rise to the
rush of the window wind and
then hearing it be taken away,
left behind in your
wake.

It feels good.

I love Jed, but I am not in love with him.
It took us a little while to figure this out.
Putting aside the fact that he's as gay as the day is long,
it would be too easy to mistake what we have for desire.

It is not desire.

Instead it is something deeper. I don't want to be with him
constantly and forever. I want to be with him for the moment,
and I want the moments to go on forever.

There is a Polaroid of him and Daniel taped to the dashboard, right next
to the clock. They are on a ferry, the sea behind them. Jed leaning
his shoulder over so Daniel can lean down into him. That wistful lucky
happiness on their faces.

I was worried at first.
Worried for Jed, yes.
But also worried for me.
He'd dated other boys,
but Daniel was something else.
He realized that from the beginning.

193

I didn't want him to be hurt.
I didn't want him to leave me.

You will always be my always, he
assured me.

And I believed him, because he'd
never given me reason not to.

(If I'd wanted to sleep with him, I
think it would've been different.)

The three of us do not go out very often
as the three of us. I think Daniel is perfect
for Jed, which is the highest compliment
I can give. But my friendship isn't with him,
and Jed understands that. When we hit the road,
we hit it together alone.

We get to the bridge, our undestined destination. Even though there's no sign,
no arrow, Jed turns at the last minute and parks us in a verge right before the
bridge leaves the ground.
The trunk pops open, and Jed runs round back to retrieve a bag of oranges
and a sweatshirt of his that fits me better.

Shall we make like lizards and leap? he asks.

I have never felt the urge to jump off a bridge,
but there are times I have wanted to jump
out of my life,
out of my skin.

Would you stroll me down the promenade instead? I ask back.

He offers his arm and says, **Most certainly, my splendid.**

I am surprised there's a sidewalk—the bridge stretches between two points of nowhere, there are no other pedestrians in sight. The walkway is narrow—if Jed and I walk side by side, one of us ends up right in the lap of the traffic.

Make way for ducklings, I suggest.

I fall back, follow him. I like for him to be in front, because that way I can watch his hair blowing wild, the bag of oranges swaying, the lift of his shoes. When I'm not looking at him, I look at the river running beneath us, its own stream of traffic.

There is no word for our kind of friendship. Two people who don't see each other a lot, but can make each other effortlessly happy.

We stop at the center.
I don't know how he determines it,
but when I look,
both ends appear to be
the same distance away.

We sit on the walkway
and dangle our legs through the railings,
kicking the air.

As he peels me an orange, he asks, **If I tell you something startling, do you promise not to swoon?**

I nod, and watch the orange peels fall to the river.

I've gotten him a ring, he says.

It wasn't until Jed that I understood how a person could be *disarming*. I have spent years of my life sitting in my room, creating defenses of cynicism, darkness, and bleakness. Jed's friendship is the skeleton key to my fortress. He disarms me every time.

Let me see it, I reply.

He hands me the open orange, sections pulled back like petals. He wipes his fingers, then carefully reaches into his pocket. What emerges is a claddagh.

Two hands, one heart.

I have seen the rings before, but never like this. Never held between two fingers instead of worn on one. Never in the windblown sun, never so high over the water. Never so close to me.

Two hands, one heart.

Do the two hands belong to two different people? Are they holding their love in common, keeping it perfectly balanced? Or do the two hands belong to one person, giving the heart as an offering *(take this, it's yours)*?

At that moment, a truck speeds across the bridge. It comes dangerously close to us and shakes the false ground that we sit on.

I am jolted forward, into the rail.

The orange falls from my hand.

And the word I think is *precarious*. Because as the bridge rocks like a beast with a
tremor down its spine, as I pitch forward so close to the air of no return, I am
struck
by how precarious it all is. How the things that hold us are only as strong
as
the faith we have in them—
you go on the bridge because you trust it will not
fall
the fingers will clasp because we trust them to.

You need two hands to hold a heart.

The tremors subside and I look over to Jed. He is ghostly
pale, but the ring is still between his forefinger and thumb.
He has held on, because he could not consider letting go.

How precarious, I say.

And he says, **You mean precious.**

He gives the ring to me, and I hold a small part of his future in my palm.

You trust me that much? I ask.

He smiles and says, **I do.**

Possibility

Here's what I know about the realm of possibility—
it is always expanding, it is never what you think
it is. Everything around us was once deemed
impossible. From the airplane overhead to
the phones in our pockets to the choir girl
putting her arm around the metalhead.
As hard as it is for us to see sometimes, we all exist
within the realm of possibility. Most of the limits
are of our own world's devising. And yet,
every day we each do so many things
that were once impossible to us.

There are hundreds of reasons for Daniel and me
to be impossible. History has not been kind
to two boys who love each other like we do.
But putting that aside. And not even considering
the fact that a hundred and fifty years ago,
his family was in a small town in Russia
and my family was in a similarly small town
in Ireland—I can't imagine they could have
imagined us here, together. Forgetting our gender,
ignoring all the strange roads that led to us
being in the same time and place, there is still
the simple impossibility of love. That all of our
contradicting securities and insecurities,

interests and disinterests, beliefs and doubts
could somehow translate into this common
uncommon affection should be as impossible
as walking to the moon. But instead, I love him.

When everybody knows you, it is easy
to think that nobody will ever really know you.
With the boy before Daniel, I could only feel
the limits. I found myself cordoning off parts of me,
saying so much less than I wanted to say.
When Daniel came into my life, the doors
inside me were still locked. I wanted to be
careful. I think our first true recognition
was our mutual hesitation, our own need to be
gradual. I liked him a lot, and was sure
it wouldn't last. I couldn't believe in it
because I was afraid to damage my faith.
Every time you love someone, you put not just
your faith in them, but your faith in everything
to the test. I didn't think I was ready for that.

On our fourth date, something changed.
Impossible to fully describe, possible
to tell. We went to a movie, and as soon
as the theater went dark, all I was aware of
was him next to me. I looked out the corner
of my eye and thought he was transfixed
by the movie. I wanted to touch him, to hold
his hand, but had no way to be sure

if it was the right thing to do. Slowly I inched
my hand towards him, right to the edge
of my seat. For a moment, I found nothing but
air. Then, gently, the side of his hand
touched the side of my hand. We both looked
down and realized we had each done
the same thing. We were equally scared
and equally longing. Somehow we knew that
my palm would turn and his palm would hover,
until we were ready for that touch, that
breathing through fingertips, that closeness
that can only come when you give it.

It has been a year now. The most understandable
thing in the world should be how minutes lead to
hours, how hours lead to days, how days can make
a year. And yet, this neat progression can still be
surprising. A year seems too monumental for us
to have reached, and at the same time too small
to contain all the minutes and hours and days
we've had together. We set each month down
like a marker beside the road, small anniversaries
with the feeling of always moving forward.

It took me a while to get used to this.
There were so many other people in my life.
I had spent all of my time listening,
learning the longings we all have in common.
I never took the time to hear them in myself

until I heard them speaking to him.
That desire for desire, that hope
for hope, the possibility of everything
truly possible. I had so many friends,
so many nods and conversations,
so many things I'd always wanted
to say to someone.

Twelve markers beside the road.
His shoelaces always on the verge
of being untied; a Pez dispenser
bought after curfew in a vast supermarket;
the pair of pants I was wearing when he first
took them off; a photo of the two of us
balanced on the seesaw in our park;
the check that caused us to scream
in argument over whose turn it was
to pay; a box of cigarettes that lasted;
the glow of the dashboard lights
on his face as he slept on my shoulder;
a mix of songs that have the words
"All I Want" in the title; the notebook I keep
of our ticket stubs; the valentine
he made by drawing a heart on his palm;
his name in my handwriting;
my name in his.

These things do not matter
except that they matter to us.

We have given them meaning
in the same way that we have given
each other meaning.

It took me ten months to know
we would make it to a year.
Most songs that begin with "All I Want"
end with "Is You"—it took me
a few verses, but eventually I got there.

How do you commemorate a year?
A paper anniversary, but we are
the words written down, not the paper.
If I could, I would give him
a lime-green couch, a cabin by a lake,
a fireworks display, an orchard of butterflies,
and the certainty that I love him.

There is certainty in a ring.
The non-ending, the non-beginning.
The ongoing.
The way it holds on to you
not because it's been fastened
or stretched or adhered.
It holds on
because it fits.

I told him I was going to the city
to see a show with my grandmother.

But instead I walked from shop to shop
looking among the glass-case rows
until I found the claddagh,
the two hands, the heart,
and I knew there was no better way
to say what I meant to say
about what he meant to me.

I wasn't thinking of marriage, just commitment.
I wasn't thinking of forever, just reveling in now.
We don't know yet how long we're meant to be—
there are so many obstacles down the road.
But there is also possibility; the ring marks the realm
of possibility.

There are times when we are sharing a pillow
that I feel such joy, bewildering joy.

Our anniversary is a Friday
and I am nervous all through school.
People know it's a big day, and they celebrate.
I guess Daniel and I have
talked about it enough that they know
the exact date, and most of the details.
I feel the ring in my pocket,
marker of my anticipation
for tonight, for beyond tonight.
Can he sense the tiny added weight
in my pocket? I don't think

we will ever want to know each other
that well, beyond surprise.

Years into days.
Days into hours.
Hours into minutes.
Minutes into moments.
Moments into possibility.

I catch him breaking into my locker,
filling it with birds in flight,
copied from photographs that were copied
from life; later I will see
there is a poem on the back of each wing.
Poems that are not about us,
but are about trees and teacups,
fields and glances. Not about us,
but about the things we hold dear.
The moments we both collect
by living our lives, together and alone.
Rearranged alphabets, dream-remnant wonder,
the seat of our love. I pretend
I don't see him kneeling there,
my own scotch-tape sweetheart.
I walk wide in my happiness
until I find the hall empty, Daniel's affection
waiting to be opened.

I spend the day withholding,

not giving him a thing
but thanks. He says I look
like someone holding flowers
behind his back. I offer my hands,
smile at their emptiness, feel
the ring pulse in my pocket,
half-expecting it to glow
like I do.

Daniel looks a little bit happy and a little bit
afraid, not that I've forgotten, but that
it might not mean as much to me, that today
will betray our unequal affections.
We have never figured out whether I need
to be more reassuring or if he just needs
reassurances too much. We both try
to readjust our settings to make it
okay. He trusts me but doesn't always
trust our love or himself. I hand him
my invisible bouquet of flowers, tell him
to wait and see, see and wait.

I have no plan. After school,
I lead him to my car, holding his hand
as we walk through the parking lot,
not brave or crazy, just in love.
I walk around to his side of the car
to unlock his door, open it for him.
He asks me where we're going

and I tell him that we'll be driving
through our story for a little bit.

After that fourth date, after our bodies
finally touched, we drove around for hours,
one hand on the steering wheel, the other
in his hand, gliding over his arm,
reaching in the headlight echo to feel
the curve of his face, his shoulder.
Pulling over to the side of the road
for that first blind, intimate kiss,
then talking past midnight as the hours
trickled away like miles. A great distance
covered, made familiar.

We cannot help but retrace those steps
as I drive without a plan. If we wanted to,
we could be in Montreal in eight hours
or Florida in a little over a day. We could
stop at dozens of houses and find our friends.
There are so many directions we could take,
but instead I keep us close. And as I do, I begin
to tell Daniel my version. I am taking him
back to the moment in art class that we first
noticed each other, I am telling him that
the whole time I was talking about the surrealists
I was wondering what it would be like
to run my hand down his back, to be able
to tell him the truth. I conjure our first date,

our second, our fourth. He tries to stop me.
As much as he seeks reassurance, he hates
being talked about. But I tell him this is a part of it,
what I want to give him on our anniversary.
I want him to know.

You think you know your possibilities.
Then other people come into your life
and suddenly there are so many more.

The whole time I've been talking, the radio
has remained silent. I've loaded the disc changer
with mixes set at random, so when I press play,
the result is a collage of our knowing references,
raspberry swirl and a case of you,
as cool as I am and galileo,
the places you have come to fear the most,
lucky denver mint, wonderwall,
all I want is you.

We live along to these songs,
sing our parts, split sometimes
into harmony and melody.
We watch our town recede, return
as I wind us through the streets,
down the roads, past the lanes.
I drive until the dimming of the day.

In the twilight, I lead us to the park
where not that long ago, I folded
a ring for him out of the cellophane
of a cigarette wrapper. I have seen it
in his drawer, in the esoteric
treasure-chest ashtray that holds
so many of our mementos. This time
I will give him a ring he can wear,
something that doesn't need to be protected
to last.

A year. A thousand kisses. And now
a thousand one, a thousand two.
There are so many other places
we could have ended up, but I have to believe
none of them would have felt this right.
All I want is you
is not entirely true.
I want so much more,
and with Daniel I think
I can get it. I tell him this,
I tell him *I love you,*
which says everything
and is entirely true.

I reach into my pocket and pull out the ring.
There is still enough light in the air
for the silver to glimmer
and his eyes to gleam.

We do not say anything,
we look at each other,
take each other in
as far as vision can go.
I hold his hand in mine,
and then with the other hand
move the non-ending, non-beginning,
ongoing ring onto his finger,
whispering my love.

We embrace.
And then the strangest,
most beautiful thing happens.
Daniel looks at the ring
and walks behind me.
Before I can figure out
what's going on,
he reaches his arms
around me, his mouth
by my ear, his chest
against my back.
He takes his hands
and forms his fingers
in the shape of a heart,
which he places over
my own heart,
whispering his love.

I wrap my arms
behind me,
hold him.
We stand there,
breathing
together.

Moments into minutes.
Minutes into hours.
Hours into days.
Days into years.
Years into possibility.

This will linger.

david levithan
is the author of *Boy Meets Boy*.
He lives in New Jersey, which is, as everyone knows,
the *real* realm of possibility.

To find out more about him, check:
www.davidlevithan.com.